WOMEN
WHO
WROTE

WOMEN
WHO
WROTE

Stories and Poems from Audacious Literary Mavens

BIOGRAPHIES BY
DANA CHAMBLEE
CARPENTER

HARPER MUSE

Editor's note: In order to preserve the authenticity of these works, many old, variant spellings (and misspellings) of words have been maintained. We have made only minor adjustments to punctuation uses in order to improve readability.

All stories, plays, and poems are in the public domain.

Biographies written by Dana Chamblee Carpenter.

Interior design by Emily Ghattas.

Published by Harper Muse, an imprint of HarperCollins Focus LLC.

ISBN 978-1-4003-4183-2 (softcover)
ISBN 978-0-7852-3627-6 (e-book)
ISBN 978-0-7852-3638-2 (downloadable audio)

Library of Congress Cataloging-in-Publication Data

CIP data is available upon request.

Printed in the United States of America
23 24 25 26 27 LBC 5 4 3 2 1

Stories

POEMS

STORIES

JANE AUSTEN

*E*veryone thinks they know Jane Austen. We read her novels again and again. We watch countless film and television adaptations and eagerly await new ones. But the Jane Austen we *think* we know is a character as carefully crafted as Elizabeth Bennet.

The fictionalization started the moment the world was introduced to Jane Austen—at her death. All the novels published during her lifetime were done so anonymously. A woman writing novels in the nineteenth century was scandalous. Excepting a few members of the aristocracy who knew her secret, the world first met a Jane Austen decidedly cut and pasted by her siblings after her death.

Her sister, Cassandra, burned most of Austen's letters and censored others by cutting out passages that apparently spoke too sharply about family or neighbors. And, in his biographical note included in the posthumous publishing of *Persuasion* and *Northanger Abbey*, her brother, Henry, gives a first and long-defining portrait of the author that implies she was a quiet, contented sister who never wanted fame and never really cared about publishing. He suggests her work was the result of genius rather than deliberate craft or intentional artistry. For decades, the only material we had to sketch our portrait of Jane Austen was strictly controlled by her loving but socially conscious family. Over time, however, earlier drafts of Austen's work and some of the surviving letters filtered into the public domain, and we came to realize the fault in our understanding of the beloved author.

The evidence is clear—Jane Austen most certainly cared about publication and making money from her work. She spent years honing her craft and revising her manuscripts, complained about low advances, and even fired off an angry missive to a publisher who had bought the rights to an early draft (of what would become *Pride and Prejudice*) but who had done nothing with the book for years. Austen demanded her copyright back. She was keenly aware of the financial precariousness of her situation after her father's death and seemingly turned to her pen in search of security and independence. She also chafed at the demands of domestic responsibilities and thanks her sister for relieving her of many of these in order for her to have time to write.

In many ways, we've always known this sharp-witted, independent, and determined woman who sees the world in puzzle pieces and herself as the visionary to put it all together. In her novels, she gives herself the power to both reflect *what is* with unabashed honesty and to subversively hint at *what might be* through her nuanced criticism of the economics of marriage (and its consequences for women), the failings of the church, and the emptiness of a propped-up gentility. We need only look past her romanticized ghost and beyond the always emphasized romances that are the heart but not the meat and bones of her stories. She's painted her own portrait in every labored-over word, in every reworked plot, in every detailed character come to life.

Jane Austen waits for us there in her novels.

LOVE AND FREINDSHIP

To Madame La Comtesse De Feuillide
This Novel Is Inscribed by Her Obliged
Humble Servant the Author.
"Deceived in Freindship and Betrayed in Love."

Letter the First

From Isabel to Laura

How often, in answer to my repeated intreaties that you would give my Daughter a regular detail of the Misfortunes and Adventures of your Life, have you said "No, my freind never will I comply with your request till I may be no longer in Danger of again experiencing such dreadful ones."

Surely that time is now at hand. You are this day 55. If a

woman may ever be said to be in safety from the determined
Perseverance of disagreeable Lovers and the cruel Persecutions
of obstinate Fathers, surely it must be at such a time of Life.

Isabel

Letter 2nd

Laura to Isabel

Altho' I cannot agree with you in supposing that I shall
never again be exposed to Misfortunes as unmerited as those
I have already experienced, yet to avoid the imputation of
Obstinacy or ill-nature, I will gratify the curiosity of your
daughter; and may the fortitude with which I have suffered
the many afflictions of my past Life, prove to her a useful les-
son for the support of those which may befall her in her own.

Laura

Letter 3rd

Laura to Marianne

As the Daughter of my most intimate freind I think you
entitled to that knowledge of my unhappy story, which your

Mother has so often solicited me to give you. My Father was a native of Ireland and an inhabitant of Wales; my Mother was the natural Daughter of a Scotch Peer by an italian Opera-girl—I was born in Spain and received my Education at a Convent in France.

When I had reached my eighteenth Year I was recalled by my Parents to my paternal roof in Wales. Our mansion was situated in one of the most romantic parts of the Vale of Uske. Tho' my Charms are now considerably softened and somewhat impaired by the Misfortunes I have undergone, I was once beautiful. But lovely as I was the Graces of my Person were the least of my Perfections. Of every accomplishment accustomary to my sex, I was Mistress. When in the Convent, my progress had always exceeded my instructions, my Acquirements had been wonderfull for my age, and I had shortly surpassed my Masters.

In my Mind, every Virtue that could adorn it was centered; it was the Rendez-vous of every good Quality and of every noble sentiment. A sensibility too tremblingly alive to every affliction of my Freinds, my Acquaintance and particularly to every affliction of my own, was my only fault, if a fault it could be called. Alas! how altered now! Tho' indeed my own Misfortunes do not make less impression on me than they ever did, yet now I never feel for those of an other. My accomplishments too, begin to fade—I can neither sing so well nor Dance so gracefully as I once did—and I have entirely forgot the MINUET DELA COUR. Adeiu.

Laura

Letter 4th

Laura to Marianne

Our neighbourhood was small, for it consisted only of your Mother. She may probably have already told you that being left by her Parents in indigent Circumstances she had retired into Wales on eoconomical motives. There it was our freindship first commenced. Isobel was then one and twenty. Tho' pleasing both in her Person and Manners (between ourselves) she never possessed the hundredth part of my Beauty or Accomplishments. Isabel had seen the World. She had passed 2 Years at one of the first Boarding-schools in London; had spent a fortnight in Bath and had supped one night in Southampton.

"Beware my Laura (she would often say) Beware of the insipid Vanities and idle Dissipations of the Metropolis of England; Beware of the unmeaning Luxuries of Bath and of the stinking fish of Southampton."

"Alas! (exclaimed I) how am I to avoid those evils I shall never be exposed to? What probability is there of my ever tasting the Dissipations of London, the Luxuries of Bath, or the stinking Fish of Southampton? I who am doomed to waste my Days of Youth and Beauty in an humble Cottage in the Vale of Uske."

Ah! little did I then think I was ordained so soon to quit that humble Cottage for the Deceitfull Pleasures of the World. Adeiu.

Laura

Letter 5th

Laura to Marianne

One Evening in December as my Father, my Mother and myself, were arranged in social converse round our Fireside, we were on a sudden greatly astonished, by hearing a violent knocking on the outward door of our rustic Cot.

My Father started—"What noise is that," (said he.) "It sounds like a loud rapping at the door"—(replied my Mother.) "it does indeed." (cried I.) "I am of your opinion; (said my Father) it certainly does appear to proceed from some uncommon violence exerted against our unoffending door." "Yes (exclaimed I) I cannot help thinking it must be somebody who knocks for admittance."

"That is another point (replied he;) We must not pretend to determine on what motive the person may knock—tho' that someone DOES rap at the door, I am partly convinced."

Here, a 2d tremendous rap interrupted my Father in his speech, and somewhat alarmed my Mother and me.

"Had we better not go and see who it is? (said she) the servants are out." "I think we had." (replied I.) "Certainly, (added my Father) by all means." "Shall we go now?" (said my Mother,) "The sooner the better." (answered he.) "Oh! let no time be lost" (cried I.)

A third more violent Rap than ever again assaulted our ears. "I am certain there is somebody knocking at the Door." (said my

Mother.) "I think there must," (replied my Father) "I fancy the servants are returned; (said I) I think I hear Mary going to the Door." "I'm glad of it (cried my Father) for I long to know who it is."

I was right in my conjecture; for Mary instantly entering the Room, informed us that a young Gentleman and his Servant were at the door, who had lossed their way, were very cold and begged leave to warm themselves by our fire.

"Won't you admit them?" (said I.) "You have no objection, my Dear?" (said my Father.) "None in the World." (replied my Mother.)

Mary, without waiting for any further commands immediately left the room and quickly returned introducing the most beauteous and amiable Youth, I had ever beheld. The servant she kept to herself.

My natural sensibility had already been greatly affected by the sufferings of the unfortunate stranger and no sooner did I first behold him, than I felt that on him the happiness or Misery of my future Life must depend. Adeiu.

Laura

Letter 6th

Laura to Marianne

The noble Youth informed us that his name was Lindsay—for particular reasons however I shall conceal it under that of Talbot.

He told us that he was the son of an English Baronet, that his Mother had been for many years no more and that he had a Sister of the middle size. "My Father (he continued) is a mean and mercenary wretch—it is only to such particular freinds as this Dear Party that I would thus betray his failings. Your Virtues my amiable Polydore (addressing himself to my father) yours Dear Claudia and yours my Charming Laura call on me to repose in you, my confidence." We bowed. "My Father seduced by the false glare of Fortune and the Deluding Pomp of Title, insisted on my giving my hand to Lady Dorothea. No never exclaimed I. Lady Dorothea is lovely and Engaging; I prefer no woman to her; but know Sir, that I scorn to marry her in compliance with your Wishes. No! Never shall it be said that I obliged my Father."

We all admired the noble Manliness of his reply. He continued.

"Sir Edward was surprised; he had perhaps little expected to meet with so spirited an opposition to his will. "Where, Edward in the name of wonder (said he) did you pick up this unmeaning gibberish? You have been studying Novels I suspect." I scorned to answer: it would have been beneath my dignity. I mounted my Horse and followed by my faithful William set forth for my Aunts."

"My Father's house is situated in Bedfordshire, my Aunt's in Middlesex, and tho' I flatter myself with being a tolerable proficient in Geography, I know not how it happened, but I found myself entering this beautifull Vale which I find is in South Wales, when I had expected to have reached my Aunts."

"After having wandered some time on the Banks of the Uske without knowing which way to go, I began to lament my cruel Destiny in the bitterest and most pathetic Manner. It was now perfectly dark, not a single star was there to direct my steps, and I know not what might have befallen me had I not at length discerned thro' the solemn Gloom that surrounded me a distant light, which as I approached it, I discovered to be the chearfull Blaze of your fire. Impelled by the combination of Misfortunes under which I laboured, namely Fear, Cold and Hunger I hesitated not to ask admittance which at length I have gained; and now my Adorable Laura (continued he taking my Hand) when may I hope to receive that reward of all the painfull sufferings I have undergone during the course of my attachment to you, to which I have ever aspired. Oh! when will you reward me with Yourself?"

"This instant, Dear and Amiable Edward." (replied I.) We were immediately united by my Father, who tho' he had never taken orders had been bred to the Church. Adeiu.

Laura

Letter 7th

Laura to Marianne

We remained but a few days after our Marriage, in the Vale of Uske. After taking an affecting Farewell of my Father, my Mother and my Isabel, I accompanied Edward to his Aunt's in Middlesex. Philippa received us both with every expression of affectionate Love. My arrival was indeed a most agreable surprise to her as she had not only been totally ignorant of my Marriage with her Nephew, but had never even had the slightest idea of there being such a person in the World.

Augusta, the sister of Edward was on a visit to her when we arrived. I found her exactly what her Brother had described her to be—of the middle size. She received me with equal surprise though not with equal Cordiality, as Philippa. There was a disagreable coldness and Forbidding Reserve in her reception of me which was equally distressing and Unexpected. None of that interesting Sensibility or amiable simpathy in her manners and Address to me when we first met which should have distinguished our introduction to each other. Her Language was neither warm, nor affectionate, her expressions of regard were neither animated nor cordial; her arms were not opened to receive me to her Heart, tho' my own were extended to press her to mine.

A short Conversation between Augusta and her Brother, which I accidentally overheard encreased my dislike to her, and convinced me that her Heart was no more formed for the soft ties of Love than for the endearing intercourse of Freindship.

"But do you think that my Father will ever be reconciled to this imprudent connection?" (said Augusta.)

"Augusta (replied the noble Youth) I thought you had

a better opinion of me, than to imagine I would so abjectly degrade myself as to consider my Father's Concurrence in any of my affairs, either of Consequence or concern to me. Tell me Augusta with sincerity; did you ever know me consult his inclinations or follow his Advice in the least trifling Particular since the age of fifteen?"

"Edward (replied she) you are surely too diffident in your own praise. Since you were fifteen only! My Dear Brother since you were five years old, I entirely acquit you of ever having willingly contributed to the satisfaction of your Father. But still I am not without apprehensions of your being shortly obliged to degrade yourself in your own eyes by seeking a support for your wife in the Generosity of Sir Edward."

"Never, never Augusta will I so demean myself. (said Edward). Support! What support will Laura want which she can receive from him?"

"Only those very insignificant ones of Victuals and Drink." (answered she.)

"Victuals and Drink! (replied my Husband in a most nobly contemptuous Manner) and dost thou then imagine that there is no other support for an exalted mind (such as is my Laura's) than the mean and indelicate employment of Eating and Drinking?"

"None that I know of, so efficacious." (returned Augusta).

"And did you then never feel the pleasing Pangs of Love,

Augusta? (replied my Edward). Does it appear impossible to your vile and corrupted Palate, to exist on Love? Can you not conceive the Luxury of living in every distress that Poverty can inflict, with the object of your tenderest affection?"

"You are too ridiculous (said Augusta) to argue with; perhaps however you may in time be convinced that . . ."

Here I was prevented from hearing the remainder of her speech, by the appearance of a very Handsome young Woman, who was ushured into the Room at the Door of which I had been listening. On hearing her announced by the Name of "Lady Dorothea," I instantly quitted my Post and followed her into the Parlour, for I well remembered that she was the Lady, proposed as a Wife for my Edward by the Cruel and Unrelenting Baronet.

Altho' Lady Dorothea's visit was nominally to Philippa and Augusta, yet I have some reason to imagine that (acquainted with the Marriage and arrival of Edward) to see me was a principal motive to it.

I soon perceived that tho' Lovely and Elegant in her Person and tho' Easy and Polite in her Address, she was of that inferior order of Beings with regard to Delicate Feeling, tender Sentiments, and refined Sensibility, of which Augusta was one.

She staid but half an hour and neither in the Course of her Visit, confided to me any of her secret thoughts, nor requested me to confide in her, any of Mine. You will easily imagine therefore my Dear Marianne that I could not feel any ardent affection or very sincere Attachment for Lady Dorothea. Adeiu.

Laura

Letter 8th

Laura to Marianne, in Continuation

Lady Dorothea had not left us long before another visitor as unexpected a one as her Ladyship, was announced. It was Sir Edward, who informed by Augusta of her Brother's marriage, came doubtless to reproach him for having dared to unite himself to me without his Knowledge. But Edward foreseeing his design, approached him with heroic fortitude as soon as he entered the Room, and addressed him in the following Manner.

"Sir Edward, I know the motive of your Journey here— You come with the base Design of reproaching me for having entered into an indissoluble engagement with my Laura without your Consent. But Sir, I glory in the Act—. It is my greatest boast that I have incurred the displeasure of my Father!"

So saying, he took my hand and whilst Sir Edward, Philippa, and Augusta were doubtless reflecting with admiration on his undaunted Bravery, led me from the Parlour to his Father's Carriage which yet remained at the Door and in which we were instantly conveyed from the pursuit of Sir Edward.

The Postilions had at first received orders only to take the London road; as soon as we had sufficiently reflected However, we ordered them to Drive to M—. the seat of Edward's most particular freind, which was but a few miles distant.

At M—. we arrived in a few hours; and on sending in our names were immediately admitted to Sophia, the Wife of Edward's freind. After having been deprived during the course of 3 weeks of a real freind (for such I term your Mother) imagine my transports at beholding one, most truly worthy of the Name. Sophia was rather above the middle size; most elegantly formed. A soft languor spread over her lovely features, but increased their Beauty—. It was the Charectarestic of her Mind—. She was all sensibility and Feeling. We flew into each others arms and after having exchanged vows of mutual Freindship for the rest of our Lives, instantly unfolded to each other the most inward secrets of our Hearts—. We were interrupted in the delightfull Employment by the entrance of Augustus, (Edward's freind) who was just returned from a solitary ramble.

Never did I see such an affecting Scene as was the meeting of Edward and Augustus.

"My Life! my Soul!" (exclaimed the former) "My adorable angel!" (replied the latter) as they flew into each other's arms.

It was too pathetic for the feelings of Sophia and myself—We
fainted alternately on a sofa. Adeiu.

Laura

Letter the 9th

From the Same to the Same

Towards the close of the day we received the following
Letter from Philippa.

"Sir Edward is greatly incensed by your abrupt departure;
he has taken back Augusta to Bedfordshire. Much as I wish
to enjoy again your charming society, I cannot determine to
snatch you from that, of such dear and deserving Freinds—
When your Visit to them is terminated, I trust you will return
to the arms of your" "Philippa."

We returned a suitable answer to this affectionate Note
and after thanking her for her kind invitation assured her that
we would certainly avail ourselves of it, whenever we might
have no other place to go to. Tho' certainly nothing could to
any reasonable Being, have appeared more satisfactory, than so
gratefull a reply to her invitation, yet I know not how it was,
but she was certainly capricious enough to be displeased with
our behaviour and in a few weeks after, either to revenge our
Conduct, or releive her own solitude, married a young and

illiterate Fortune-hunter. This imprudent step (tho' we were sensible that it would probably deprive us of that fortune which Philippa had ever taught us to expect) could not on our own accounts, excite from our exalted minds a single sigh; yet fearfull lest it might prove a source of endless misery to the deluded Bride, our trembling Sensibility was greatly affected when we were first informed of the Event. The affectionate Entreaties of Augustus and Sophia that we would for ever consider their House as our Home, easily prevailed on us to determine never more to leave them, In the society of my Edward and this Amiable Pair, I passed the happiest moments of my Life; Our time was most delightfully spent, in mutual Protestations of Freindship, and in vows of unalterable Love, in which we were secure from being interrupted, by intruding and disagreable Visitors, as Augustus and Sophia had on their first Entrance in the Neighbourhood, taken due care to inform the surrounding Families, that as their happiness centered wholly in themselves, they wished for no other society. But alas! my Dear Marianne such Happiness as I then enjoyed was too perfect to be lasting. A most severe and unexpected Blow at once destroyed every sensation of Pleasure. Convinced as you must be from what I have already told you concerning Augustus and Sophia, that there never were a happier Couple, I need not I imagine, inform you that their union had been contrary to the inclinations of their Cruel and Mercenery Parents; who had vainly endeavoured with obstinate Perseverance to force them into a Marriage with those whom they had ever abhorred; but with a Heroic Fortitude worthy to be related and admired, they had both, constantly refused to submit to such despotic Power.

After having so nobly disentangled themselves from the shackles of Parental Authority, by a Clandestine Marriage, they were determined never to forfeit the good opinion they had gained in the World, in so doing, by accepting any proposals of reconciliation that might be offered them by their Fathers—to this farther tryal of their noble independance however they never were exposed.

They had been married but a few months when our visit to them commenced during which time they had been amply supported by a considerable sum of money which Augustus had gracefully purloined from his unworthy father's Escritoire, a few days before his union with Sophia.

By our arrival their Expenses were considerably encreased tho' their means for supplying them were then nearly exhausted. But they, Exalted Creatures! scorned to reflect a moment on their pecuniary Distresses and would have blushed at the idea of paying their Debts.—Alas! what was their Reward for such disinterested Behaviour! The beautifull Augustus was arrested and we were all undone. Such perfidious Treachery in the merciless perpetrators of the Deed will shock your gentle nature Dearest Marianne as much as it then affected the Delicate sensibility of Edward, Sophia, your Laura, and of Augustus himself. To compleat such unparalelled Barbarity we were informed that an Execution in the House would shortly take place. Ah! what could we do but what we did! We sighed and fainted on the sofa. Adeiu.

Laura

Letter 10th

Laura in Continuation

When we were somewhat recovered from the over-powering Effusions of our grief, Edward desired that we would consider what was the most prudent step to be taken in our unhappy situation while he repaired to his imprisoned freind to lament over his misfortunes. We promised that we would, and he set forwards on his journey to Town. During his absence we faithfully complied with his Desire and after the most mature Deliberation, at length agreed that the best thing we could do was to leave the House; of which we every moment expected the officers of Justice to take possession. We waited therefore with the greatest impatience, for the return of Edward in order to impart to him the result of our Deliberations. But no Edward appeared. In vain did we count the tedious moments of his absence—in vain did we weep—in vain even did we sigh—no Edward returned—. This was too cruel, too unexpected a Blow to our Gentle Sensibility—we could not support it—we could only faint. At length collecting all the Resolution I was Mistress of, I arose and after packing up some necessary apparel for Sophia and myself, I dragged her to a Carriage I had ordered and we instantly set out for London. As the Habitation of Augustus was within twelve miles of Town, it was not long e'er we arrived there, and no sooner had we entered Holboun than letting down one of the Front Glasses I enquired of every decent-looking Person that we passed "If they had seen my Edward?"

But as we drove too rapidly to allow them to answer my repeated Enquiries, I gained little, or indeed, no information concerning him. "Where am I to drive?" said the Postilion. "To Newgate Gentle Youth (replied I), to see Augustus." "Oh! no, no, (exclaimed Sophia) I cannot go to Newgate; I shall not be able to support the sight of my Augustus in so cruel a confinement—my feelings are sufficiently shocked by the RECITAL, of his Distress, but to behold it will overpower my Sensibility." As I perfectly agreed with her in the Justice of her Sentiments the Postilion was instantly directed to return into the Country. You may perhaps have been somewhat surprised my Dearest Marianne, that in the Distress I then endured, destitute of any support, and unprovided with any Habitation, I should never once have remembered my Father and Mother or my paternal Cottage in the Vale of Uske. To account for this seeming forgetfullness I must inform you of a trifling circumstance concerning them which I have as yet never mentioned.

The death of my Parents a few weeks after my Departure, is the circumstance I allude to. By their decease I became the lawfull Inheritress of their House and Fortune. But alas! the House had never been their own and their Fortune had only been an Annuity on their own Lives. Such is the Depravity of the World! To your Mother I should have returned with Pleasure, should have been happy to have introduced to her, my charming Sophia and should with Chearfullness have passed the remainder of my Life in their dear Society in the Vale of Uske, had not one obstacle to the execution of so agreable a scheme, intervened; which was the Marriage and Removal of your Mother to a distant part of Ireland. Adeiu.

Laura

Letter 11th

Laura in Continuation

"I have a Relation in Scotland (said Sophia to me as we left London) who I am certain would not hesitate in receiving me." "Shall I order the Boy to drive there?" said I—but instantly recollecting myself, exclaimed, "Alas I fear it will be too long a Journey for the Horses." Unwilling however to act only from my own inadequate Knowledge of the Strength and Abilities of Horses, I consulted the Postilion, who was

entirely of my Opinion concerning the Affair. We therefore
determined to change Horses at the next Town and to travel
Post the remainder of the Journey—. When we arrived at the
last Inn we were to stop at, which was but a few miles from the
House of Sophia's Relation, unwilling to intrude our Society
on him unexpected and unthought of, we wrote a very elegant
and well penned Note to him containing an account of our
Destitute and melancholy Situation, and of our intention to
spend some months with him in Scotland. As soon as we
had dispatched this Letter, we immediately prepared to fol-
low it in person and were stepping into the Carriage for that
Purpose when our attention was attracted by the Entrance
of a coroneted Coach and 4 into the Inn-yard. A Gentleman
considerably advanced in years descended from it. At his first
Appearance my Sensibility was wonderfully affected and e'er
I had gazed at him a 2d time, an instinctive sympathy whis-
pered to my Heart, that he was my Grandfather. Convinced
that I could not be mistaken in my conjecture I instantly
sprang from the Carriage I had just entered, and following
the Venerable Stranger into the Room he had been shewn
to, I threw myself on my knees before him and besought
him to acknowledge me as his Grand Child. He started, and
having attentively examined my features, raised me from the
Ground and throwing his Grand-fatherly arms around my
Neck, exclaimed, "Acknowledge thee! Yes dear resemblance
of my Laurina and Laurina's Daughter, sweet image of my

Claudia and my Claudia's Mother, I do acknowledge thee as the Daughter of the one and the Grandaughter of the other." While he was thus tenderly embracing me, Sophia astonished at my precipitate Departure, entered the Room in search of me. No sooner had she caught the eye of the venerable Peer, than he exclaimed with every mark of Astonishment— "Another Grandaughter! Yes, yes, I see you are the Daughter of my Laurina's eldest Girl; your resemblance to the beauteous Matilda sufficiently proclaims it. "Oh!" replied Sophia, "when I first beheld you the instinct of Nature whispered me that we were in some degree related—But whether Grandfathers, or Grandmothers, I could not pretend to determine." He folded her in his arms, and whilst they were tenderly embracing, the Door of the Apartment opened and a most beautifull young Man appeared. On perceiving him Lord St. Clair started and retreating back a few paces, with uplifted Hands, said, "Another Grand-child! What an unexpected Happiness is this! to discover in the space of 3 minutes, as many of my Descendants! This I am certain is Philander the son of my Laurina's 3d girl the amiable Bertha; there wants now but the presence of Gustavus to compleat the Union of my Laurina's Grand-Children."

"And here he is; (said a Gracefull Youth who that instant entered the room) here is the Gustavus you desire to see. I am the son of Agatha your Laurina's 4th and youngest Daughter," "I see you are indeed; replied Lord St. Clair—But tell me (continued he looking fearfully towards the Door) tell me, have I any other Grand-children in the House." "None my Lord." "Then I will provide for you all without farther delay— Here are 4 Banknotes of 50L each—Take them and remember I have done the Duty of a Grandfather." He instantly left the Room and immediately afterwards the House. Adeiu.

Laura

Letter the 12th

Laura in Continuation

You may imagine how greatly we were surprised by the sudden departure of Lord St Clair. "Ignoble Grand-sire!" exclaimed Sophia. "Unworthy Grandfather!" said I, and instantly fainted in each other's arms. How long we remained in this situation I know not; but when we recovered we found ourselves alone, without either Gustavus, Philander, or the Banknotes. As we were deploring our unhappy fate, the Door of the Apartment opened and "Macdonald" was announced. He was Sophia's cousin. The haste with which he came to our releif so soon after the receipt of our Note, spoke so greatly in his favour that I hesitated not to pronounce him at first sight, a tender and simpathetic Freind. Alas! he little deserved the name—for though he told us that he was much concerned at our Misfortunes, yet by his own account it appeared that the perusal of them, had neither drawn from him a single sigh, nor induced him to bestow one curse on our vindictive stars—. He told Sophia that his Daughter depended on her returning with him to Macdonald-Hall, and that as his Cousin's freind he should be happy to see me there also. To Macdonald-Hall, therefore we went, and were received with great kindness by Janetta the Daughter of Macdonald, and the Mistress of the Mansion. Janetta was then only fifteen; naturally well disposed, endowed with a susceptible Heart, and a simpathetic Disposition, she might, had these amiable qualities been properly encouraged, have been an ornament to human Nature; but unfortunately her Father possessed not a soul sufficiently exalted to admire so promising a Disposition, and had endeavoured by every means on his power to prevent it encreasing with her Years. He had actually so far extinguished the natural noble Sensibility of her Heart, as to prevail on her to accept an offer from a young Man of his Recommendation. They were to be married in a few months, and Graham, was in the House when we arrived. WE soon saw through his character. He was just such a Man as one might have expected to be the choice of Macdonald. They said he was Sensible, well-informed, and Agreable; we did not pretend to Judge of such trifles, but as we were convinced he had no soul, that he had never read the sorrows of Werter, and that his Hair bore not the least resemblance to auburn, we were certain that Janetta could feel no affection for him, or at least that she ought to feel none. The very circumstance of his being her father's choice too, was so much in his disfavour, that had he been deserving her, in every other respect yet THAT of itself ought to have been a sufficient reason in the Eyes of Janetta for rejecting him. These considerations we were determined to represent to her in their proper light and doubted not of meeting with the desired success from one naturally so well disposed; whose errors in the affair had only arisen from a want of proper confidence in her own opinion, and a suitable contempt of her father's. We found her indeed all that our warmest wishes could have hoped for; we had no difficulty to convince her that it was impossible she could love Graham, or that it was her Duty to disobey her Father; the only thing at which she rather seemed to hesitate was our assertion that she must be attached to some other Person. For some time, she persevered in declaring that she knew no other young man for whom she had the the smallest Affection; but upon explaining the impossibility of such a thing she said that she beleived she DID LIKE Captain M'Kenrie better than any one she knew besides. This confession satisfied us and after having enumerated the good Qualities of M'Kenrie and assured her that she was violently in love with him, we desired to know whether he had ever in any wise declared his affection to her.

"So far from having ever declared it, I have no reason to

imagine that he has ever felt any for me." said Janetta. "That he certainly adores you (replied Sophia) there can be no doubt—. The Attachment must be reciprocal. Did he never gaze on you with admiration—tenderly press your hand—drop an involantary tear—and leave the room abruptly?" "Never (replied she) that I remember—he has always left the room indeed when his visit has been ended, but has never gone away particularly abruptly or without making a bow." Indeed my Love (said I) you must be mistaken—for it is absolutely impossible that he should ever have left you but with Confusion, Despair, and Precipitation. Consider but for a moment Janetta, and you must be convinced how absurd it is to suppose that he could ever make a Bow, or behave like any other Person." Having settled this Point to our satisfaction, the next we took into consideration was, to determine in what manner we should inform M'Kenrie of the favourable Opinion Janetta entertained of him. . . . We at length agreed to acquaint him with it by an anonymous Letter which Sophia drew up in the following manner.

"Oh! happy Lover of the beautifull Janetta, oh! amiable Possessor of HER Heart whose hand is destined to another, why do you thus delay a confession of your attachment to the amiable Object of it? Oh! consider that a few weeks will at once put an end to every flattering Hope that you may now entertain, by uniting the unfortunate Victim of her father's Cruelty to the execrable and detested Graham."

"Alas! why do you thus so cruelly connive at the projected Misery of her and of yourself by delaying to communicate that scheme which had doubtless long possessed your imagination? A secret Union will at once secure the felicity of both."

The amiable M'Kenrie, whose modesty as he afterwards assured us had been the only reason of his having so long concealed the violence of his affection for Janetta, on receiving this Billet flew on the wings of Love to Macdonald-Hall, and so powerfully pleaded his Attachment to her who inspired it, that after a few more private interveiws, Sophia and I experienced the satisfaction of seeing them depart for Gretna-Green, which they chose for the celebration of their Nuptials, in preference to any other place although it was at a considerable distance from Macdonald-Hall. Adeiu.

Laura

Letter the 13th

Laura in Continuation

They had been gone nearly a couple of Hours, before either Macdonald or Graham had entertained any suspicion of the affair. And they might not even then have suspected it, but for the following little Accident. Sophia happening one day to open a private Drawer in Macdonald's Library with one of her own keys, discovered that it was the Place where he kept his Papers of consequence and amongst them some bank notes of considerable amount. This discovery she imparted to me; and having agreed together that it would be a proper treatment of so vile a Wretch as Macdonald to deprive him of money, perhaps dishonestly gained, it was determined that the next time we should either of us happen to go that way, we would take one or more of the Bank notes from the drawer. This well meant Plan we had often successfully put in Execution; but alas! on the very day of Janetta's Escape, as Sophia was majestically removing the 5th Bank-note from the Drawer to her own purse, she was suddenly most impertinently interrupted in her employment by the entrance of Macdonald himself, in a most abrupt and precipitate Manner. Sophia (who though naturally all winning sweetness could when occasions demanded it call forth the Dignity of her sex) instantly put on a most forbidding look, and darting an angry frown on the undaunted culprit, demanded in a haughty tone of voice "Wherefore her retirement was thus insolently broken in on?" The unblushing Macdonald, without even endeavouring to exculpate himself from the crime he was charged with, meanly endeavoured to reproach Sophia with ignobly defrauding him of his money . . . The dignity of Sophia was wounded; "Wretch (exclaimed she, hastily replacing the Bank-note in the Drawer) how darest thou to accuse me of an Act, of which the bare idea makes me blush?" The base wretch was still unconvinced and continued to upbraid the justly-offended Sophia in such opprobious Language, that at length he so greatly provoked the gentle sweetness of her Nature, as to induce her to revenge herself on him by informing him of Janetta's Elopement, and of the active Part we had both taken in the affair. At this period of their Quarrel I entered the Library and was as you may imagine equally offended as Sophia at the ill-grounded accusations of the malevolent and contemptible Macdonald. "Base Miscreant! (cried I) how canst thou thus undauntedly endeavour to sully the spotless reputation of such bright Excellence? Why dost thou not suspect MY innocence as soon?" "Be satisfied Madam (replied he) I DO suspect it, and therefore must desire that you will both leave this House in less than half an hour."

"We shall go willingly; (answered Sophia) our hearts have long detested thee, and nothing but our freindship for thy Daughter could have induced us to remain so long beneath thy roof."

"Your Freindship for my Daughter has indeed been most powerfully exerted by throwing her into the arms of an unprincipled Fortune-hunter." (replied he.)

"Yes, (exclaimed I) amidst every misfortune, it will afford us some consolation to reflect that by this one act of Freindship to Janetta, we have amply discharged every obligation that we have received from her father."

"It must indeed be a most gratefull reflection, to your exalted minds." (said he.)

As soon as we had packed up our wardrobe and valuables, we left Macdonald Hall, and after having walked about a mile and a half we sate down by the side of a clear limpid stream to refresh our exhausted limbs. The place was suited to meditation. A grove of full-grown Elms sheltered us from the East—. A Bed of full-grown Nettles from the West—. Before us ran the murmuring brook and behind us ran the turn-pike road. We were in a mood for contemplation and in a Disposition to enjoy so beautifull a spot. A mutual silence which had for some time reigned between us, was at length broke by my exclaiming—"What a lovely scene! Alas why are not Edward and Augustus here to enjoy its Beauties with us?"

"Ah! my beloved Laura (cried Sophia) for pity's sake forbear recalling to my remembrance the unhappy situation of my imprisoned Husband. Alas, what would I not give to learn the fate of my Augustus! to know if he is still in Newgate, or if he is yet hung. But never shall I be able so far to conquer my tender sensibility as to enquire after him. Oh! do not I beseech you ever let me again hear you repeat his beloved name—. It affects me too deeply—. I cannot bear to hear him mentioned it wounds my feelings."

"Excuse me my Sophia for having thus unwillingly offended you—" replied I—and then changing the conversation, desired her to admire the noble Grandeur of the Elms which sheltered us from the Eastern Zephyr. "Alas! my Laura (returned she) avoid so melancholy a subject, I intreat you.

Do not again wound my Sensibility by observations on those elms. They remind me of Augustus. He was like them, tall, magestic—he possessed that noble grandeur which you admire in them."

I was silent, fearfull lest I might any more unwillingly distress her by fixing on any other subject of conversation which might again remind her of Augustus.

"Why do you not speak my Laura? (said she after a short pause) "I cannot support this silence you must not leave me to my own reflections; they ever recur to Augustus."

"What a beautifull sky! (said I) How charmingly is the azure varied by those delicate streaks of white!"

"Oh! my Laura (replied she hastily withdrawing her Eyes from a momentary glance at the sky) do not thus distress me by calling my Attention to an object which so cruelly reminds me of my Augustus's blue sattin waistcoat striped in white! In pity to your unhappy freind avoid a subject so distressing." What could I do? The feelings of Sophia were at that time so exquisite, and the tenderness she felt for Augustus so poignant that I had not power to start any other topic, justly fearing that it might in some unforseen manner again awaken all her sensibility by directing her thoughts to her Husband. Yet to be silent would be cruel; she had intreated me to talk.

From this Dilemma I was most fortunately releived by an accident truly apropos; it was the lucky overturning of a Gentleman's Phaeton, on the road which ran murmuring behind us. It was a most fortunate accident as it diverted the attention of Sophia from the melancholy reflections which she had been before indulging. We instantly quitted our seats and ran to the rescue of those who but a few moments before had been in so elevated a situation as a fashionably high Phaeton, but who were now laid low and sprawling in the Dust. "What an ample subject for reflection on the uncertain Enjoyments of this World, would not that Phaeton and the Life of Cardinal Wolsey afford a thinking Mind!" said I to Sophia as we were hastening to the field of Action.

She had not time to answer me, for every thought was now engaged by the horrid spectacle before us. Two Gentlemen most elegantly attired but weltering in their blood was what first struck our Eyes—we approached—they were Edward and Augustus—. Yes dearest Marianne they were our Husbands. Sophia shreiked and fainted on the ground—I screamed and instantly ran mad—. We remained thus mutually deprived of our senses, some minutes, and on regaining them were deprived of them again. For an Hour and a Quarter did we continue in this unfortunate situation—Sophia fainting every moment and I running mad as often. At length a groan from the hapless Edward (who alone retained any share of life) restored us to ourselves. Had we indeed before imagined that either of them lived, we should have been more sparing of our Greif—but as we had supposed when we first beheld them that they were no more, we knew that nothing could remain to be done but what we were about. No sooner did we therefore hear my Edward's groan than postponing our lamentations for the present, we hastily ran to the Dear Youth and kneeling on each side of him implored him not to die—. "Laura (said He fixing his now languid Eyes on me) I fear I have been overturned."

I was overjoyed to find him yet sensible.

"Oh! tell me Edward (said I) tell me I beseech you before you die, what has befallen you since that unhappy Day in which Augustus was arrested and we were separated—"

"I will" (said he) and instantly fetching a deep sigh, Expired—. Sophia immediately sank again into a swoon—. MY greif was more audible. My Voice faltered, My Eyes assumed a vacant stare, my face became as pale as Death, and my senses were considerably impaired—. "Talk not to me of Phaetons (said I, raving in a frantic, incoherent manner)—Give me a violin—. I'll play to him and sooth him in his melancholy Hours—Beware ye gentle Nymphs of Cupid's Thunderbolts, avoid the piercing shafts of Jupiter—Look at that grove of Firs—I see a Leg of Mutton—They told me Edward was not Dead; but they deceived me—they took him for a cucumber—" Thus I continued wildly exclaiming on my Edward's Death—. For two Hours did I rave thus madly and should not then have left off, as I was not in the least fatigued, had not Sophia who was just recovered from her swoon, intreated me to consider that Night was now approaching and that the Damps began to fall. "And whither shall we go (said I) to shelter us from either?" "To that white Cottage." (replied she pointing to a neat Building which rose up amidst the grove of Elms and which I had not before observed—) I agreed and we instantly walked to it—we knocked at the door—it was opened by an old woman; on being requested to afford us a Night's Lodging, she informed us that her House was but small, that she had only two Bedrooms, but that However we should be wellcome to one of them. We were satisfied and followed the good woman into the House where we were greatly cheered by the sight of a comfortable fire—. She was a widow and had only one Daughter, who was then just seventeen—One of the best of ages; but alas! she was very plain and her name was Bridget. . . . Nothing therfore could be expected from her—she could not be supposed to possess either exalted Ideas, Delicate Feelings or refined Sensibilities—. She was nothing more than a mere good-tempered, civil and obliging young woman; as such we could scarcely dislike here—she was only an Object of Contempt—. Adeiu.

Laura

Letter the 14th

Laura in Continuation

Arm yourself my amiable young Freind with all the philosophy you are Mistress of; summon up all the fortitude you possess, for alas! in the perusal of the following Pages your sensibility will be most severely tried. Ah! what were the misfortunes I had before experienced and which I have already related to you, to the one I am now going to inform you of. The Death of my Father and my Mother and my Husband though almost more than my gentle Nature could support, were trifles in comparison to the misfortune I am now proceeding to relate. The morning after our arrival at the Cottage, Sophia complained of a violent pain in her delicate limbs, accompanied with a disagreable Head-ake She attributed it to a cold caught by her continued faintings in the open air as the Dew was falling the Evening before. This I feared was but too probably the case; since how could it be otherwise accounted for that I should have escaped the same indisposition, but by supposing that the bodily Exertions I had undergone in my repeated fits of frenzy had so effectually circulated and warmed my Blood as to make me proof against the chilling Damps of Night, whereas, Sophia lying totally inactive on the ground must have been exposed to all their severity. I was most seriously alarmed by her illness which trifling as it may appear to you, a certain instinctive sensibility whispered me, would in the End be fatal to her.

Alas! my fears were but too fully justified; she grew gradually worse—and I daily became more alarmed for her. At length she was obliged to confine herself solely to the Bed allotted us by our worthy Landlady—. Her disorder turned

to a galloping Consumption and in a few days carried her off.
Amidst all my Lamentations for her (and violent you may
suppose they were) I yet received some consolation in the
reflection of my having paid every attention to her, that could
be offered, in her illness. I had wept over her every Day—had
bathed her sweet face with my tears and had pressed her fair
Hands continually in mine—. "My beloved Laura (said she
to me a few Hours before she died) take warning from my
unhappy End and avoid the imprudent conduct which had
occasioned it . . . Beware of fainting-fits . . . Though at the
time they may be refreshing and agreable yet beleive me they
will in the end, if too often repeated and at improper seasons,
prove destructive to your Constitution . . . My fate will teach
you this. I die a Martyr to my greif for the loss of Augustus.
One fatal swoon has cost me my Life. Beware of swoons Dear
Laura. . . . A frenzy fit is not one quarter so pernicious; it is
an exercise to the Body and if not too violent, is I dare say
conducive to Health in its consequences—Run mad as often
as you chuse; but do not faint—"

These were the last words she ever addressed to me. It
was her dieing Advice to her afflicted Laura, who has ever
most faithfully adhered to it.

After having attended my lamented freind to her Early
Grave, I immediately (tho' late at night) left the detested
Village in which she died, and near which had expired my
Husband and Augustus. I had not walked many yards from

it before I was overtaken by a stage-coach, in which I instantly took a place, determined to proceed in it to Edinburgh, where I hoped to find some kind some pitying Freind who would receive and comfort me in my afflictions.

It was so dark when I entered the Coach that I could not distinguish the Number of my Fellow-travellers; I could only perceive that they were many. Regardless however of anything concerning them, I gave myself up to my own sad Reflections. A general silence prevailed—A silence, which was by nothing interrupted but by the loud and repeated snores of one of the Party.

"What an illiterate villain must that man be! (thought I to myself) What a total want of delicate refinement must he have, who can thus shock our senses by such a brutal noise! He must I am certain be capable of every bad action! There is no crime too black for such a Character!" Thus reasoned I within myself, and doubtless such were the reflections of my fellow travellers.

At length, returning Day enabled me to behold the unprincipled Scoundrel who had so violently disturbed my feelings. It was Sir Edward the father of my Deceased Husband. By his side sate Augusta, and on the same seat with me were your Mother and Lady Dorothea. Imagine my surprise at finding myself thus seated amongst my old Acquaintance. Great as was my astonishment, it was yet increased, when on looking out of Windows, I beheld the Husband of Philippa, with Philippa by his side, on the Coachbox and when on looking behind I beheld, Philander and Gustavus in the Basket. "Oh!

Heavens, (exclaimed I) is it possible that I should so unexpect-
edly be surrounded by my nearest Relations and Connections?"
These words roused the rest of the Party, and every eye was
directed to the corner in which I sat. "Oh! my Isabel (continued
I throwing myself across Lady Dorothea into her arms) receive
once more to your Bosom the unfortunate Laura. Alas! when
we last parted in the Vale of Usk, I was happy in being united
to the best of Edwards; I had then a Father and a Mother,
and had never known misfortunes—But now deprived of every
freind but you—"

"What! (interrupted Augusta) is my Brother dead then?
Tell us I intreat you what is become of him?" "Yes, cold and
insensible Nymph, (replied I) that luckless swain your Brother,
is no more, and you may now glory in being the Heiress of Sir
Edward's fortune."

Although I had always despised her from the Day I had
overheard her conversation with my Edward, yet in civility I
complied with hers and Sir Edward's intreaties that I would
inform them of the whole melancholy affair. They were
greatly shocked—even the obdurate Heart of Sir Edward
and the insensible one of Augusta, were touched with sorrow,
by the unhappy tale. At the request of your Mother I related
to them every other misfortune which had befallen me since
we parted. Of the imprisonment of Augustus and the absence
of Edward—of our arrival in Scotland—of our unexpected
Meeting with our Grand-father and our cousins—of our visit

to Macdonald-Hall—of the singular service we there per-
formed towards Janetta—of her Fathers ingratitude for it. of
his inhuman Behaviour, unaccountable suspicions, and barba-
rous treatment of us, in obliging us to leave the House. of our
lamentations on the loss of Edward and Augustus and finally
of the melancholy Death of my beloved Companion.

Pity and surprise were strongly depictured in your
Mother's countenance, during the whole of my narration, but
I am sorry to say, that to the eternal reproach of her sensibility,
the latter infinitely predominated. Nay, faultless as my conduct
had certainly been during the whole course of my late mis-
fortunes and adventures, she pretended to find fault with my
behaviour in many of the situations in which I had been placed.
As I was sensible myself, that I had always behaved in a man-
ner which reflected Honour on my Feelings and Refinement,
I paid little attention to what she said, and desired her to
satisfy my Curiosity by informing me how she came there,
instead of wounding my spotless reputation with unjustifiable
Reproaches. As soon as she had complied with my wishes in
this particular and had given me an accurate detail of every
thing that had befallen her since our separation (the particulars
of which if you are not already acquainted with, your Mother
will give you) I applied to Augusta for the same information
respecting herself, Sir Edward and Lady Dorothea.

She told me that having a considerable taste for the
Beauties of Nature, her curiosity to behold the delightful

scenes it exhibited in that part of the World had been so
much raised by Gilpin's Tour to the Highlands, that she had
prevailed on her Father to undertake a Tour to Scotland
and had persuaded Lady Dorothea to accompany them.
That they had arrived at Edinburgh a few Days before and
from thence had made daily Excursions into the Country
around in the Stage Coach they were then in, from one of
which Excursions they were at that time returning. My next
enquiries were concerning Philippa and her Husband, the
latter of whom I learned having spent all her fortune, had
recourse for subsistence to the talent in which, he had always
most excelled, namely, Driving, and that having sold every
thing which belonged to them except their Coach, had con-
verted it into a Stage and in order to be removed from any of
his former Acquaintance, had driven it to Edinburgh from
whence he went to Sterling every other Day. That Philippa
still retaining her affection for her ungratefull Husband, had
followed him to Scotland and generally accompanied him in
his little Excursions to Sterling. "It has only been to throw
a little money into their Pockets (continued Augusta) that
my Father has always travelled in their Coach to veiw the
beauties of the Country since our arrival in Scotland—for
it would certainly have been much more agreable to us, to
visit the Highlands in a Postchaise than merely to travel
from Edinburgh to Sterling and from Sterling to Edinburgh
every other Day in a crowded and uncomfortable Stage." I

perfectly agreed with her in her sentiments on the affair, and secretly blamed Sir Edward for thus sacrificing his Daughter's Pleasure for the sake of a ridiculous old woman whose folly in marrying so young a man ought to be punished. His Behaviour however was entirely of a peice with his general Character; for what could be expected from a man who possessed not the smallest atom of Sensibility, who scarcely knew the meaning of simpathy, and who actually snored—. Adeiu.

Laura

Letter the 15th

Laura in Continuation

When we arrived at the town where we were to Breakfast, I was determined to speak with Philander and Gustavus, and to that purpose as soon as I left the Carriage, I went to the Basket and tenderly enquired after their Health, expressing my fears of the uneasiness of their situation. At first they seemed rather confused at my appearance dreading no doubt that I might call them to account for the money which our Grandfather had left me and which they had unjustly deprived me of, but finding that I mentioned nothing of the Matter, they desired me to step into the Basket as we might there converse with greater ease. Accordingly I entered and whilst the rest of the party were devouring green tea and buttered toast, we feasted ourselves in a more refined and sentimental Manner by a confidential Conversation. I informed them of every thing which had befallen me during the course of my life, and at my request they related to me every incident of theirs.

"We are the sons as you already know, of the two youngest Daughters which Lord St Clair had by Laurina an italian opera girl. Our mothers could neither of them exactly ascertain who were our Father, though it is generally beleived that Philander, is the son of one Philip Jones a Bricklayer and that my Father was one Gregory Staves a Staymaker of Edinburgh. This is however of little consequence for as our Mothers were certainly never married to either of them it reflects no Dishonour on our Blood, which is of a most ancient and unpolluted kind. Bertha (the Mother of Philander) and Agatha (my own Mother) always lived together. They were neither of them very rich; their united fortunes had originally amounted to nine thousand Pounds, but as they had always lived on the principal of it, when we were fifteen it was diminished to nine Hundred. This nine Hundred they always kept in a Drawer in one of the Tables which stood in our common sitting Parlour, for the convenience of having it always at Hand. Whether it was from this circumstance, of its being easily taken, or from a wish of being independant, or from an excess of sensibility (for which we were always remarkable) I cannot now determine, but certain it is that when we had reached our 15th year, we took the nine Hundred Pounds and ran away. Having obtained this prize we were determined to manage it with eoconomy and not to spend it either with folly or Extravagance. To this purpose we therefore divided it into nine parcels, one of which we devoted to Victuals, the 2d to Drink, the 3d to Housekeeping, the 4th to Carriages, the 5th to Horses, the 6th to Servants, the 7th to Amusements, the 8th to Cloathes and the 9th to Silver Buckles. Having thus arranged our Expences for two months (for we expected to make the nine Hundred Pounds last as long) we hastened to London and had the good luck to spend it in 7 weeks and a Day which was 6 Days sooner than we had intended. As soon as we had thus happily disencumbered ourselves from the weight of so much money, we began to think of returning to our Mothers, but accidentally hearing that they were both starved to Death, we gave over the design and determined to engage ourselves to some strolling Company of Players, as we had always a turn for the Stage. Accordingly we offered our services to one and were accepted; our Company was indeed rather small, as it consisted only of the Manager his wife and ourselves, but there were fewer to pay and the only inconvenience attending it was the Scarcity of Plays which for want of People to fill the Characters, we could perform. We did not mind trifles however—. One of our most admired Performances was MACBETH, in which we were truly great. The Manager always played BANQUO himself, his Wife my LADY MACBETH. I did the THREE WITCHES and Philander acted ALL THE REST. To say the truth this tragedy was not only the Best, but the only Play that we ever performed; and after having acted it all over England, and Wales, we came to Scotland to exhibit it over the remainder of Great Britain. We happened to be quartered in that very Town, where you came and met your Grandfather—. We were in the Inn-yard when his Carriage entered and perceiving by the arms to whom it belonged, and knowing that Lord St Clair was our Grandfather, we agreed to endeavour to get something from him by discovering the Relationship—. You know how well it succeeded—. Having obtained the two Hundred Pounds, we instantly left the Town, leaving our Manager and his Wife to act MACBETH by themselves, and took the road to Sterling, where we spent our little fortune with great ECLAT. We are now returning to Edinburgh in order to get some preferment in the Acting way; and such my Dear Cousin is our History."

I thanked the amiable Youth for his entertaining narration, and after expressing my wishes for their Welfare and Happiness, left them in their little Habitation and returned to my other Freinds who impatiently expected me.

My adventures are now drawing to a close my dearest Marianne; at least for the present.

When we arrived at Edinburgh Sir Edward told me that

as the Widow of his son, he desired I would accept from his Hands of four Hundred a year. I graciously promised that I would, but could not help observing that the unsimpathetic Baronet offered it more on account of my being the Widow of Edward than in being the refined and amiable Laura.

I took up my Residence in a Romantic Village in the Highlands of Scotland where I have ever since continued, and where I can uninterrupted by unmeaning Visits, indulge in a melancholy solitude, my unceasing Lamentations for the Death of my Father, my Mother, my Husband and my Freind.

Augusta has been for several years united to Graham the Man of all others most suited to her; she became acquainted with him during her stay in Scotland.

Sir Edward in hopes of gaining an Heir to his Title and Estate, at the same time married Lady Dorothea—. His wishes have been answered.

Philander and Gustavus, after having raised their reputation by their Performances in the Theatrical Line at Edinburgh, removed to Covent Garden, where they still exhibit under the assumed names of LUVIS and QUICK.

Philippa has long paid the Debt of Nature, Her Husband however still continues to drive the Stage-Coach from Edinburgh to Sterling:—Adeiu my Dearest Marianne.

Laura

KATHERINE MANSFIELD

A restless soul, Katherine Mansfield spun a fragmented, frenetic, whirling dervish of a life for her short thirty-four years. Born in 1888 to prominent, wealthy parents in New Zealand who were neither indulgent nor indifferent, she knew at an early age that she was not meant for their conventional lifestyle. At ten, she set her mind to becoming a professional writer. She wrote for and edited her school paper and was criticized for a lack of charm and grace by her teachers. In her youth, she fell in love with Oscar Wilde's work (which shaped her attitudes about life) and, later, while she was attending school in London, she discovered the Russian novelists, who showed her the heights and depths of storytelling. After a short and miserable return to the slower pace of life in New Zealand (but also professionally productive as she published her first short stories), Mansfield convinced her parents to give her a living allowance and let her return to London.

Immersed in the bohemian liberalities of the day and comfortable with her own appetites, Mansfield spent her early twenties falling in and out of love with men and women, dealing with the consequences (a pregnancy she miscarried and gonorrhea), writing constantly, and rising in prominence among the London literary community. Here, she met the two people who seemed to serve as anchors for Mansfield throughout the rest of her life: Ida Baker and John Middleton Murry. She bounced between the two of them like a Ping-Pong ball, but they each provided a different degree of stability to the untethered author: Baker offered an emotional constancy and Murry, a domestic one.

The brilliance of Mansfield's writing reflects her freewheeling way of living. She shows us the same kaleidoscope world in her writing—deeply complex characters engaged in intricate psychological conflict and discovery jutted up against powerfully beautiful and symbolic natural settings, layered understandings of estrangement and longing, the varied and infinite workings of the human heart. But whereas her life twisted and twirled seemingly without reason or forethought, the expansive, penetrating worlds she crafts in her work are contained within the clarity of her words and her tight, transcendent storytelling.

THE GARDEN-PARTY

*A*nd after all the weather was ideal. They could not have had a more perfect day for a garden-party if they had ordered it. Windless, warm, the sky without a cloud. Only the blue was veiled with a haze of light gold, as it is sometimes in early summer. The gardener had been up since dawn, mowing the lawns and sweeping them, until the grass and the dark flat rosettes where the daisy plants had been seemed to shine. As for the roses, you could not help feeling they understood that roses are the only flowers that impress people at garden-parties; the only flowers that everybody is certain of knowing. Hundreds, yes, literally hundreds, had come out in a single night; the green bushes bowed down as though they had been visited by archangels.

Breakfast was not yet over before the men came to put up the marquee.

"Where do you want the marquee put, mother?"

"My dear child, it's no use asking me. I'm determined to leave everything to you children this year. Forget I am your mother. Treat me as an honoured guest."

But Meg could not possibly go and supervise the men. She had washed her hair before breakfast, and she sat drinking her coffee in a green turban, with a dark wet curl stamped on each cheek. Jose, the butterfly, always came down in a silk petticoat and a kimono jacket.

"You'll have to go, Laura; you're the artistic one."

Away Laura flew, still holding her piece of bread-and-butter. It's so delicious to have an excuse for eating out of doors, and besides, she loved having to arrange things; she always felt she could do it so much better than anybody else.

Four men in their shirt-sleeves stood grouped together on the garden path. They carried staves covered with rolls of canvas, and they had big tool-bags slung on their backs. They looked impressive. Laura wished now that she had not got the bread-and-butter, but there was nowhere to put it, and she couldn't possibly throw it away. She blushed and tried to look severe and even a little bit short-sighted as she came up to them.

"Good morning," she said, copying her mother's voice. But that sounded so fearfully affected that she was ashamed, and stammered like a little girl, "Oh—er—have you come—is it about the marquee?"

"That's right, miss," said the tallest of the men, a lanky, freckled fellow, and he shifted his tool-bag, knocked back his straw hat and smiled down at her. "That's about it."

His smile was so easy, so friendly that Laura recovered. What nice eyes he had, small, but such a dark blue! And now she looked at the others, they were smiling too. "Cheer up, we won't bite," their smile seemed to say. How very nice workmen were! And what a beautiful morning! She mustn't mention the morning; she must be business-like. The marquee.

"Well, what about the lily-lawn? Would that do?"

And she pointed to the lily-lawn with the hand that didn't hold the bread-and-butter. They turned, they stared in the direction. A little fat chap thrust out his under-lip, and the tall fellow frowned.

"I don't fancy it," said he. "Not conspicuous enough. You see, with a thing like a marquee," and he turned to Laura in his easy way, "you want to put it somewhere where it'll give you a bang slap in the eye, if you follow me."

Laura's upbringing made her wonder for a moment whether it was quite respectful of a workman to talk to her of bangs slap in the eye. But she did quite follow him.

"A corner of the tennis-court," she suggested. "But the band's going to be in one corner."

"H'm, going to have a band, are you?" said another of the workmen. He was pale. He had a haggard look as his dark eyes scanned the tennis-court. What was he thinking?

"Only a very small band," said Laura gently. Perhaps he wouldn't mind so much if the band was quite small. But the tall fellow interrupted.

"Look here, miss, that's the place. Against those trees. Over there. That'll do fine."

Against the karakas. Then the karaka-trees would be hidden. And they were so lovely, with their broad, gleaming leaves, and their clusters of yellow fruit. They were like trees you imagined growing on a desert island, proud, solitary, lifting their leaves and fruits to the sun in a kind of silent splendour. Must they be hidden by a marquee?

They must. Already the men had shouldered their staves and were making for the place. Only the tall fellow was left. He bent down, pinched a sprig of lavender, put his thumb and forefinger to his nose and snuffed up the smell. When Laura saw that gesture she forgot all about the karakas in her wonder at him caring for things like that—caring for the smell of lavender. How many men that she knew would have done such a thing? Oh, how extraordinarily nice workmen were, she thought. Why couldn't she have workmen for her friends rather than the silly boys she danced with and who came to Sunday night supper? She would get on much better with men like these.

It's all the fault, she decided, as the tall fellow drew something on the back of an envelope, something that was to be looped up or left to hang, of these absurd class distinctions. Well, for her part, she didn't feel them. Not a bit, not an atom . . . And now there came the chock-chock of wooden hammers. Some one whistled, some one sang out, "Are you right there, matey?" "Matey!" The friendliness of it, the—the—Just to prove how happy she was, just to show the tall fellow how at home she felt, and how she despised stupid conventions, Laura took a big bite of her bread-and-butter as she stared at the little drawing. She felt just like a work-girl.

"Laura, Laura, where are you? Telephone, Laura!" a voice cried from the house.

"Coming!" Away she skimmed, over the lawn, up the path, up the steps, across the veranda, and into the porch. In the hall her father and Laurie were brushing their hats ready to go to the office.

"I say, Laura," said Laurie very fast, "you might just give a squiz at my coat before this afternoon. See if it wants pressing."

"I will," said she. Suddenly she couldn't stop herself. She ran at Laurie and gave him a small, quick squeeze. "Oh, I do love parties, don't you?" gasped Laura.

"Ra-ther," said Laurie's warm, boyish voice, and he squeezed his sister too, and gave her a gentle push. "Dash off to the telephone, old girl."

The telephone. "Yes, yes; oh yes. Kitty? Good morning, dear. Come to lunch? Do, dear. Delighted of course. It will only be a very scratch meal—just the sandwich crusts and broken meringue-shells and what's left over. Yes, isn't it a perfect morning? Your white? Oh, I certainly should. One moment—hold the line. Mother's calling." And Laura sat back. "What, mother? Can't hear."

Mrs. Sheridan's voice floated down the stairs. "Tell her to wear that sweet hat she had on last Sunday."

"Mother says you're to wear that sweet hat you had on last Sunday. Good. One o'clock. Bye-bye."

Laura put back the receiver, flung her arms over her head, took a deep breath, stretched and let them fall. "Huh," she sighed, and the moment after the sigh she sat up quickly. She was still, listening. All the doors in the house seemed to be open. The house was alive with soft, quick steps and running voices. The green baize door that led to the kitchen regions swung open and shut with a muffled thud. And now there came a long, chuckling absurd sound. It was the heavy piano being moved on its stiff castors. But the air! If you stopped to notice, was the air always like this? Little faint winds were playing chase, in at the tops of the windows, out at the doors. And there were two tiny spots of sun, one on the inkpot, one on a silver photograph frame, playing too. Darling little spots. Especially the one on the inkpot lid. It was quite warm. A warm little silver star. She could have kissed it.

The front door bell pealed, and there sounded the rustle of Sadie's print skirt on the stairs. A man's voice murmured; Sadie answered, careless, "I'm sure I don't know. Wait. I'll ask Mrs Sheridan."

"What is it, Sadie?" Laura came into the hall.

"It's the florist, Miss Laura."

It was, indeed. There, just inside the door, stood a wide, shallow tray full of pots of pink lilies. No other kind. Nothing but lilies—canna lilies, big pink flowers, wide open, radiant, almost frighteningly alive on bright crimson stems.

"O-oh, Sadie!" said Laura, and the sound was like a little moan. She crouched down as if to warm herself at that blaze of lilies; she felt they were in her fingers, on her lips, growing in her breast.

"It's some mistake," she said faintly. "Nobody ever ordered so many. Sadie, go and find mother."

But at that moment Mrs. Sheridan joined them.

"It's quite right," she said calmly. "Yes, I ordered them. Aren't they lovely?" She pressed Laura's arm. "I was passing the shop yesterday, and I saw them in the window. And I suddenly thought for once in my life I shall have enough canna lilies. The garden-party will be a good excuse."

"But I thought you said you didn't mean to interfere," said Laura. Sadie had gone. The florist's man was still outside at his van. She put her arm round her mother's neck and gently, very gently, she bit her mother's ear.

"My darling child, you wouldn't like a logical mother, would you? Don't do that. Here's the man."

He carried more lilies still, another whole tray.

"Bank them up, just inside the door, on both sides of the porch, please," said Mrs. Sheridan. "Don't you agree, Laura?"

"Oh, I do, mother."

In the drawing-room Meg, Jose and good little Hans had at last succeeded in moving the piano.

"Now, if we put this chesterfield against the wall and move everything out of the room except the chairs, don't you think?"

"Quite."

"Hans, move these tables into the smoking-room, and bring a sweeper to take these marks off the carpet and—one moment, Hans—" Jose loved giving orders to the servants, and they loved obeying her. She always made them feel they were taking part in some drama. "Tell mother and Miss Laura to come here at once."

"Very good, Miss Jose."

She turned to Meg. "I want to hear what the piano sounds like, just in case I'm asked to sing this afternoon. Let's try over 'This life is Weary.'"

Pom! Ta-ta-ta Tee-ta! The piano burst out so passionately that Jose's face changed. She clasped her hands. She looked mournfully and enigmatically at her mother and Laura as they came in.

"This Life is Wee-ary, A Tear-a Sigh. A Love that Chan-ges, This Life is Wee-ary, A Tear-a Sigh. A Love that Chan-ges, And then . . . Good-bye!"

But at the word "Good-bye," and although the piano sounded more desperate than ever, her face broke into a brilliant, dreadfully unsympathetic smile.

"Aren't I in good voice, mummy?" she beamed.

"This Life is Wee-ary, Hope comes to Die. A Dream-a Wa-kening."

But now Sadie interrupted them. "What is it, Sadie?"

"If you please, m'm, cook says have you got the flags for the sandwiches?"

"The flags for the sandwiches, Sadie?" echoed Mrs. Sheridan dreamily. And the children knew by her face that she hadn't got them. "Let me see." And she said to Sadie firmly, "Tell cook I'll let her have them in ten minutes."

Sadie went.

"Now, Laura," said her mother quickly, "come with me into the smoking-room. I've got the names somewhere on the back of an envelope. You'll have to write them out for me. Meg, go upstairs this minute and take that wet thing off your head. Jose, run and finish dressing this instant. Do you hear me, children, or shall I have to tell your father when he comes home to-night? And-and, Jose, pacify cook if you do go into the kitchen, will you? I'm terrified of her this morning."

The envelope was found at last behind the dining-room clock, though how it had got there Mrs. Sheridan could not imagine.

"One of you children must have stolen it out of my bag, because I remember vividly—cream cheese and lemon-curd. Have you done that?"

"Yes."

"Egg and—" Mrs. Sheridan held the envelope away from her. "It looks like mice. It can't be mice, can it?"

"Olive, pet," said Laura, looking over her shoulder.

"Yes, of course, olive. What a horrible combination it sounds. Egg and olive."

They were finished at last, and Laura took them off to the kitchen. She found Jose there pacifying the cook, who did not look at all terrifying.

"I have never seen such exquisite sandwiches," said Jose's rapturous voice. "How many kinds did you say there were, cook? Fifteen?"

"Fifteen, Miss Jose."

"Well, cook, I congratulate you."

Cook swept up crusts with the long sandwich knife, and smiled broadly.

"Godber's has come," announced Sadie, issuing out of the pantry. She had seen the man pass the window.

That meant the cream puffs had come. Godber's were famous for their cream puffs. Nobody ever thought of making them at home.

"Bring them in and put them on the table, my girl," ordered cook.

Sadie brought them in and went back to the door. Of course Laura and Jose were far too grown-up to really care about such things. All the same, they couldn't help agreeing that the puffs looked very attractive. Very. Cook began arranging them, shaking off the extra icing sugar.

"Don't they carry one back to all one's parties?" said Laura.

"I suppose they do," said practical Jose, who never liked to be carried back. "They look beautifully light and feathery, I must say."

"Have one each, my dears," said cook in her comfortable voice. "Yer ma won't know."

Oh, impossible. Fancy cream puffs so soon after breakfast. The very idea made one shudder. All the same, two minutes later Jose and Laura were licking their fingers with that absorbed inward look that only comes from whipped cream.

"Let's go into the garden, out by the back way," suggested Laura. "I want to see how the men are getting on with the marquee. They're such awfully nice men."

But the back door was blocked by cook, Sadie, Godber's man and Hans.

Something had happened.

"Tuk-tuk-tuk," clucked cook like an agitated hen. Sadie had her hand clapped to her cheek as though she had toothache. Hans's face was screwed up in the effort to understand. Only Godber's man seemed to be enjoying himself; it was his story.

"What's the matter? What's happened?"

"There's been a horrible accident," said Cook. "A man killed."

"A man killed! Where? How? When?"

But Godber's man wasn't going to have his story snatched from under his very nose.

"Know those little cottages just below here, miss?" Know them? Of course, she knew them. "Well, there's a young chap living there, name of Scott, a carter. His horse shied at a traction-engine, corner of Hawke Street this morning, and he was thrown out on the back of his head. Killed."

"Dead!" Laura stared at Godber's man.

"Dead when they picked him up," said Godber's man with relish. "They were taking the body home as I come up here." And he said to the cook, "He's left a wife and five little ones."

"Jose, come here." Laura caught hold of her sister's sleeve and dragged her through the kitchen to the other side of the green baize door. There she paused and leaned against it. "Jose!" she said, horrified, "however are we going to stop everything?"

"Stop everything, Laura!" cried Jose in astonishment. "What do you mean?"

"Stop the garden-party, of course." Why did Jose pretend?

But Jose was still more amazed. "Stop the garden-party? My dear Laura, don't be so absurd. Of course we can't do anything of the kind. Nobody expects us to. Don't be so extravagant."

"But we can't possibly have a garden-party with a man dead just outside the front gate."

That really was extravagant, for the little cottages were in a lane to themselves at the very bottom of a steep rise that led up to the house. A broad road ran between. True, they were far too near. They were the greatest possible eyesore, and they had no right to be in that neighbourhood at all. They were little mean dwellings painted a chocolate brown. In the garden patches there was nothing but cabbage stalks, sick hens and tomato cans. The very smoke coming out of their chimneys was poverty-stricken. Little rags and shreds of smoke, so unlike the great silvery plumes that uncurled from the Sheridans' chimneys. Washerwomen lived in the lane and sweeps and a cobbler, and a man whose house-front was studded all over with minute bird-cages. Children swarmed. When the Sheridans were little they were forbidden to set foot there because of the revolting language and of what they might catch. But since they were grown up, Laura and Laurie on their prowls sometimes walked through. It was disgusting and sordid. They came out with a shudder. But still one must go everywhere; one must see everything. So through they went.

"And just think of what the band would sound like to that poor woman," said Laura.

"Oh, Laura!" Jose began to be seriously annoyed. "If you're going to stop a band playing every time some one has an accident, you'll lead a very strenuous life. I'm every bit as sorry about it as you. I feel just as sympathetic." Her eyes hardened. She looked at her sister just as she used to when they were little and fighting together. "You won't bring a drunken workman back to life by being sentimental," she said softly.

"Drunk! Who said he was drunk?" Laura turned furiously

on Jose. She said, just as they had used to say on those occasions, "I'm going straight up to tell mother."

"Do, dear," cooed Jose.

"Mother, can I come into your room?" Laura turned the big glass door-knob.

"Of course, child. Why, what's the matter? What's given you such a colour?" And Mrs. Sheridan turned round from her dressing-table. She was trying on a new hat.

"Mother, a man's been killed," began Laura.

"Not in the garden?" interrupted her mother.

"No, no!"

"Oh, what a fright you gave me!" Mrs. Sheridan sighed with relief, and took off the big hat and held it on her knees.

"But listen, mother," said Laura. Breathless, half-choking, she told the dreadful story. "Of course, we can't have our party, can we?" she pleaded. "The band and everybody arriving. They'd hear us, mother; they're nearly neighbours!"

To Laura's astonishment her mother behaved just like Jose; it was harder to bear because she seemed amused. She refused to take Laura seriously.

"But, my dear child, use your common sense. It's only by accident we've heard of it. If some one had died there normally—and I can't understand how they keep alive in those poky little holes—we should still be having our party, shouldn't we?"

Laura had to say "yes" to that, but she felt it was all wrong. She sat down on her mother's sofa and pinched the cushion frill.

"Mother, isn't it terribly heartless of us?" she asked.

"Darling!" Mrs. Sheridan got up and came over to her, carrying the hat. Before Laura could stop her she had popped it on. "My child!" said her mother, "the hat is yours. It's made for you. It's much too young for me. I have never seen you look such a picture. Look at yourself!" And she held up her hand-mirror.

"But, mother," Laura began again. She couldn't look at herself; she turned aside.

This time Mrs. Sheridan lost patience just as Jose had done.

"You are being very absurd, Laura," she said coldly. "People like that don't expect sacrifices from us. And it's not very sympathetic to spoil everybody's enjoyment as you're doing now."

"I don't understand," said Laura, and she walked quickly out of the room into her own bedroom. There, quite by chance, the first thing she saw was this charming girl in the mirror, in her black hat trimmed with gold daisies, and a long black velvet ribbon. Never had she imagined she could look like that. Is mother right? she thought. And now she hoped her mother was right. Am I being extravagant? Perhaps it was extravagant. Just for a moment she had another glimpse of that poor woman and those little children, and the body being carried into the house. But it all seemed blurred, unreal, like a picture in the newspaper. I'll remember it again after the party's over, she decided. And somehow that seemed quite the best plan . . .

Lunch was over by half-past one. By half-past two they were

all ready for the fray. The green-coated band had arrived and was established in a corner of the tennis-court.

"My dear!" trilled Kitty Maitland, "aren't they too like frogs for words? You ought to have arranged them round the pond with the conductor in the middle on a leaf."

Laurie arrived and hailed them on his way to dress. At the sight of him Laura remembered the accident again. She wanted to tell him. If Laurie agreed with the others, then it was bound to be all right. And she followed him into the hall.

"Laurie!"

"Hallo!" He was half-way upstairs, but when he turned round and saw Laura he suddenly puffed out his cheeks and goggled his eyes at her. "My word, Laura! You do look stunning," said Laurie. "What an absolutely topping hat!"

Laura said faintly "Is it?" and smiled up at Laurie, and didn't tell him after all.

Soon after that people began coming in streams. The band struck up; the hired waiters ran from the house to the marquee. Wherever you looked there were couples strolling, bending to the flowers, greeting, moving on over the lawn. They were like bright birds that had alighted in the Sheridans' garden for this one afternoon, on their way to—where? Ah, what happiness it is to be with people who all are happy, to press hands, press cheeks, smile into eyes.

"Darling Laura, how well you look!"

"What a becoming hat, child!"

"Laura, you look quite Spanish. I've never seen you look so striking."

And Laura, glowing, answered softly, "Have you had tea? Won't you have an ice? The passion-fruit ices really are rather special." She ran to her father and begged him. "Daddy darling, can't the band have something to drink?"

And the perfect afternoon slowly ripened, slowly faded, slowly its petals closed.

"Never a more delightful garden-party . . ." "The greatest success . . ." "Quite the most . . ."

Laura helped her mother with the good-byes. They stood side by side in the porch till it was all over.

"All over, all over, thank heaven," said Mrs. Sheridan. "Round up the others, Laura. Let's go and have some fresh coffee. I'm exhausted. Yes, it's been very successful. But oh, these parties, these parties! Why will you children insist on giving parties!" And they all of them sat down in the deserted marquee.

"Have a sandwich, daddy dear. I wrote the flag."

"Thanks." Mr. Sheridan took a bite and the sandwich was gone. He took another. "I suppose you didn't hear of a beastly accident that happened to-day?" he said.

"My dear," said Mrs. Sheridan, holding up her hand, "we did. It nearly ruined the party. Laura insisted we should put it off."

"Oh, mother!" Laura didn't want to be teased about it.

"It was a horrible affair all the same," said Mr. Sheridan.

"The chap was married too. Lived just below in the lane, and leaves a wife and half a dozen kiddies, so they say."

An awkward little silence fell. Mrs. Sheridan fidgeted with her cup. Really, it was very tactless of father . . .

Suddenly she looked up. There on the table were all those sandwiches, cakes, puffs, all uneaten, all going to be wasted. She had one of her brilliant ideas.

"I know," she said. "Let's make up a basket. Let's send that poor creature some of this perfectly good food. At any rate, it will be the greatest treat for the children. Don't you agree? And she's sure to have neighbours calling in and so on. What a point to have it all ready prepared. Laura!" She jumped up. "Get me the big basket out of the stairs cupboard."

"But, mother, do you really think it's a good idea?" said Laura.

Again, how curious, she seemed to be different from them all. To take scraps from their party. Would the poor woman really like that?

"Of course! What's the matter with you to-day? An hour or two ago you were insisting on us being sympathetic, and now—"

Oh well! Laura ran for the basket. It was filled, it was heaped by her mother.

"Take it yourself, darling," said she. "Run down just as you are. No, wait, take the arum lilies too. People of that class are so impressed by arum lilies."

"The stems will ruin her lace frock," said practical Jose.

So they would. Just in time. "Only the basket, then. And, Laura!"—her mother followed her out of the marquee—"Don't on any account—"

"What mother?"

No, better not put such ideas into the child's head! "Nothing! Run along."

It was just growing dusky as Laura shut their garden gates. A big dog ran by like a shadow. The road gleamed white, and down below in the hollow the little cottages were in deep shade. How quiet it seemed after the afternoon. Here she was going down the hill to somewhere where a man lay dead, and she couldn't realize it. Why couldn't she? She stopped a minute. And it seemed to her that kisses, voices, tinkling spoons, laughter, the smell of crushed grass were somehow inside her. She had no room for anything else. How strange! She looked up at the pale sky, and all she thought was, "Yes, it was the most successful party."

Now the broad road was crossed. The lane began, smoky and dark. Women in shawls and men's tweed caps hurried by. Men hung over the palings; the children played in the doorways. A low hum came from the mean little cottages. In some of them there was a flicker of light, and a shadow, crab-like, moved across the window. Laura bent her head and hurried on. She wished now she had put on a coat. How her frock shone! And the big hat with the velvet streamer—if only it was another hat! Were the people looking at her? They must be. It was a mistake to have come; she knew all along it was a mistake. Should she go back even now?

No, too late. This was the house. It must be. A dark knot of people stood outside. Beside the gate an old, old woman with a crutch sat in a chair, watching. She had her feet on a newspaper. The voices stopped as Laura drew near. The group parted. It was as though she was expected, as though they had known she was coming here.

Laura was terribly nervous. Tossing the velvet ribbon over her shoulder, she said to a woman standing by, "Is this Mrs. Scott's house?" and the woman, smiling queerly, said, "It is, my lass."

Oh, to be away from this! She actually said, "Help me, God," as she walked up the tiny path and knocked. To be away from those staring eyes, or to be covered up in anything, one of those women's shawls even. I'll just leave the basket and go, she decided. I shan't even wait for it to be emptied.

Then the door opened. A little woman in black showed in the gloom.

Laura said, "Are you Mrs. Scott?" But to her horror the woman answered, "Walk in please, miss," and she was shut in the passage.

"No," said Laura, "I don't want to come in. I only want to leave this basket. Mother sent—"

The little woman in the gloomy passage seemed not to have

heard her. "Step this way, please, miss," she said in an oily voice, and Laura followed her.

She found herself in a wretched little low kitchen, lighted by a smoky lamp. There was a woman sitting before the fire.

"Em," said the little creature who had let her in. "Em! It's a young lady." She turned to Laura. She said meaningly, "I'm 'er sister, miss. You'll excuse 'er, won't you?"

"Oh, but of course!" said Laura. "Please, please don't disturb her. I-I only want to leave—"

But at that moment the woman at the fire turned round. Her face, puffed up, red, with swollen eyes and swollen lips, looked terrible. She seemed as though she couldn't understand why Laura was there. What did it mean? Why was this stranger standing in the kitchen with a basket? What was it all about? And the poor face puckered up again.

"All right, my dear," said the other. "I'll thenk the young lady."

And again she began, "You'll excuse her, miss, I'm sure," and her face, swollen too, tried an oily smile.

Laura only wanted to get out, to get away. She was back in the passage. The door opened. She walked straight through into the bedroom, where the dead man was lying.

"You'd like a look at 'im, wouldn't you?" said Em's sister, and she brushed past Laura over to the bed. "Don't be afraid, my lass,"—and now her voice sounded fond and sly, and fondly she drew down the sheet—"'e looks a picture. There's nothing to show. Come along, my dear."

Laura came.

There lay a young man, fast asleep—sleeping so soundly, so deeply, that he was far, far away from them both. Oh, so remote, so peaceful. He was dreaming. Never wake him up again. His head was sunk in the pillow, his eyes were closed; they were blind under the closed eyelids. He was given up to his dream. What did garden-parties and baskets and lace frocks matter to him? He was far from all those things. He was wonderful, beautiful. While they were laughing and while the band was playing, this marvel had come to the lane. Happy . . . happy . . . All is well, said that sleeping face. This is just as it should be. I am content.

But all the same you had to cry, and she couldn't go out of the room without saying something to him. Laura gave a loud childish sob.

"Forgive my hat," she said.

And this time she didn't wait for Em's sister. She found her way out of the door, down the path, past all those dark people. At the corner of the lane she met Laurie.

He stepped out of the shadow. "Is that you, Laura?"

"Yes."

"Mother was getting anxious. Was it all right?"

"Yes, quite. Oh, Laurie!" She took his arm, she pressed up against him.

"I say, you're not crying, are you?" asked her brother.

Laura shook her head. She was.

Laurie put his arm round her shoulder. "Don't cry," he said in his warm, loving voice. "Was it awful?"

"No," sobbed Laura. "It was simply marvellous. But Laurie—" She stopped, she looked at her brother. "Isn't life," she stammered, "isn't life—" But what life was she couldn't explain. No matter. He quite understood.

"Isn't it, darling?" said Laurie.

WILLA CATHER

*T*here's nowhere to hide on the Nebraska prairie—not from yourself, not from others. This open, expansive landscape, which so definitively shaped Willa Cather's fiction, also helped define her understanding of herself and gave her the bold clarity that cut an unfaltering path to her success.

She was born in Virginia in 1873, and her family's move to Nebraska afforded a nine-year-old Cather exposure to a diverse community of immigrants and Native Americans as well a greater liberation from social expectation. The isolation and harsh conditions of life on the prairie meant that the roles of women (and men), the distinctions of class and race, though still present in the cultural periphery, took a back seat to doing whatever was necessary to survive. Cather took that freedom and ran with it. She often went by "Willie," cut her hair short, and wore masculine-styled clothes. At eleven, she took a job delivering the mail, which gave her access to the wider community of European settlers and their cultural experiences and stories of far-off places and times past—all of which young Cather gathered like treasure, vibrant gems in a barren landscape.

In her first semester at the University of Nebraska, she decided she wanted to be a writer. And so she did, with one decided step after another, conquering the Nebraska publications first before moving on to Pittsburgh. She wrote nonfiction and poetry and short stories—whatever was necessary—and then she went to work as the managing editor at *McClure's Magazine* in New York, permanently situating herself in the heart of the literary world. It's also where she met her partner, Edith Lewis, who lived with Cather for nearly forty years and edited much of her work.

In 1912, Cather left *McClure's* because she wanted to write novels. And so she did—beautiful, unique, powerful novels about regular people living regular lives in the most extraordinary ways. Cather brings the Nebraska prairie to life and lays bare the bold truths exposed under the open sky. But the magic of her work is the subtle beauty she captures: the shifting shades of golds and yellows of infinite wheat fields, the varying songs of the prairie birds, the layered complexities of seemingly simple lives.

A Gold Slipper

Marshall McKann followed his wife and her friend Mrs. Post down the aisle and up the steps to the stage of the Carnegie Music Hall with an ill-concealed feeling of grievance. Heaven knew he never went to concerts, and to be mounted upon the stage in this fashion, as if he were a "highbrow" from Sewickley, or some unfortunate with a musical wife, was ludicrous. A man went to concerts when he was courting, while he was a junior partner. When he became a person of substance he stopped that sort of nonsense. His wife, too, was a sensible person, the daughter of an old Pittsburgh family as solid and well-rooted as the McKanns. She would never have bothered him about this concert had not the meddlesome Mrs. Post arrived to pay her a visit. Mrs. Post was an old school friend of Mrs. McKann, and because she lived in Cincinnati she was always keeping up with the world and talking about things in which no one else was interested, music among them. She was an aggressive lady, with weighty opinions, and a deep voice like a jovial bassoon. She had arrived only last night, and at dinner she brought it out that she could on no account miss Kitty Ayrshire's recital; it was, she said, the sort of thing no one could afford to miss.

When McKann went into town in the morning he found that every seat in the music-hall was sold. He telephoned his wife to that effect, and, thinking he had settled the matter, made his reservation on the 11:25 train for New York. He was unable to get a drawing-room because this same Kitty Ayrshire had taken the last one. He had not intended going to New York until the following week, but he preferred to be absent during Mrs. Post's incumbency.

In the middle of the morning, when he was deep in his correspondence, his wife called him up to say the enterprising Mrs. Post had telephoned some musical friends in Sewickley and had found that two hundred folding-chairs were to be placed on the stage of the concert-hall, behind the piano, and that they would be on sale at noon. Would he please get seats in the front row? McKann asked if they would not excuse him, since he was going over to New York on the late train, would be tired, and would not have time to dress, etc. No, not at all. It would be foolish for two women to trail up to the stage unattended. Mrs. Post's husband always accompanied her to concerts, and she expected that much attention from her host. He needn't dress, and he could take a taxi from the concert-hall to the East Liberty station.

The outcome of it all was that, though his bag was at the station, here was McKann, in the worst possible humour, facing the large audience to which he was well known, and sitting among a lot of music students and excitable old maids. Only the desperately zealous or the morbidly curious would endure two hours in those wooden chairs, and he sat in the front row of this hectic body, somehow made a party to a transaction for which he had the utmost contempt.

When McKann had been in Paris, Kitty Ayrshire was singing at the Comique, and he wouldn't go to hear her—even there, where one found so little that was better to do. She was too much talked about, too much advertised; always being thrust in an American's face as if she were something to be proud of. Perfumes and petticoats and cutlets were named for her. Some one had pointed Kitty out to him one afternoon when she was driving in the Bois with a French composer—old enough, he judged, to be her father—who was said to be infatuated, carried away by her. McKann was told that this was one of the historic passions of old age. He had looked at her on that occasion, but she was so befrilled and befeathered that he caught nothing but a graceful outline and a small, dark head above a white ostrich boa. He had noted with disgust, however, the stooped shoulders and white imperial of the silk-hatted man beside her, and the senescent line of his back. McKann described to his wife this unpleasing picture only last night, while he was undressing, when he was making every possible effort to avert this concert party.

But Bessie only looked superior and said she wished to hear Kitty Ayrshire sing, and that her "private life" was something in which she had no interest.

Well, here he was; hot and uncomfortable, in a chair much too small for him, with a row of blinding footlights glaring in his eyes. Suddenly the door at his right elbow opened. Their seats were at one end of the front row; he had thought they would be less conspicuous there than in the centre, and he had not foreseen that the singer would walk over him every time she came upon the stage. Her velvet train brushed against his trousers as she passed him. The applause which greeted her was neither overwhelming nor prolonged. Her conservative audience did not know exactly how to accept her toilette. They were accustomed to dignified concert gowns, like those which Pittsburgh matrons (in those days!) wore at their daughters' coming-out teas.

Kitty's gown that evening was really quite outrageous—the repartée of a conscienceless Parisian designer who took her hint that she wished something that would be entirely novel in the States. Today, after we have all of us, even in the uttermost provinces, been educated by Baskt and the various Ballets Russes, we would accept such a gown without distrust; but then it was a little disconcerting, even to the well-disposed. It was constructed of a yard or two of green velvet—a reviling, shrieking green which would have made a fright of any woman who had not inextinguishable beauty—and it was made without armholes, a device to which we were then so unaccustomed that it was nothing less than alarming. The velvet skirt split back from a transparent gold-lace petticoat, gold stockings, gold slippers. The narrow train was, apparently, looped to both ankles, and it kept curling about her feet like a serpent's tail, turning up its gold lining as if it were squirming over on its back. It was not, we felt, a costume in which to sing Mozart and Handel and Beethoven.

Kitty sensed the chill in the air, and it amused her. She liked to be thought a brilliant artist by other artists, but by the world at large she liked to be thought a daring creature. She had every reason to believe, from experience and from example, that to shock the great crowd was the surest way to get its money and to make her name a household word. Nobody ever became a household word of being an artist, surely; and you were not a thoroughly paying proposition until your name meant something on the sidewalk and in the barber-shop. Kitty studied her audience with an appraising eye. She liked the stimulus of this disapprobation. As she faced this hard-shelled public she felt keen and interested; she knew that she would give such a recital as cannot often be heard for money. She nodded gaily to the young man at the piano, fell into an attitude of seriousness, and began the group of Beethoven and Mozart songs.

Though McKann would not have admitted it, there were really a great many people in the concert-hall who knew what the prodigal daughter of their country was singing, and how well she was doing it. They thawed gradually under the beauty of her voice and the subtlety of her interpretation. She had sung seldom in concert then, and they had supposed her very dependent upon the accessories of the opera. Clean singing, finished artistry, were not what they expected from her. They began to feel, even, the wayward charm of her personality.

McKann, who stared coldly up at the balconies during her first song, during the second glanced cautiously at the green apparition before him. He was vexed with her for having retained a débutante figure. He comfortably classed all singers—especially operatic singers—as "fat Dutchwomen" or "shifty Sadies," and Kitty would not fit into his clever generalization. She displayed, under his nose, the only kind of figure he considered worth looking at—that of a very young girl, supple and sinuous and quicksilverish; thin, eager shoulders, polished white arms that were nowhere too fat and nowhere too thin. McKann found it agreeable to look at Kitty, but when he saw that the authoritative Mrs. Post, red as a turkey-cock with opinions she was bursting to impart, was studying and appraising the singer through her lorgnette, he gazed indifferently out into the house again. He felt for his watch, but his wife touched him warningly with her elbow—which, he noticed, was not at all like Kitty's.

When Miss Ayrshire finished her first group of songs, her audience expressed its approval positively, but guardedly. She smiled bewitchingly upon the people in front, glanced up at the balconies, and then turned to the company huddled on the stage behind her. After her gay and careless bows, she retreated toward the stage door. As she passed McKann, she again brushed lightly against him, and this time she paused long enough to glance down at him and murmur, "Pardon!"

In the moment her bright, curious eyes rested upon him, McKann seemed to see himself as if she were holding a mirror up before him. He beheld himself a heavy, solid figure, unsuitably clad for the time and place, with a florid, square face, well-visored with good living and sane opinions—an inexpressive countenance. Not a rock face, exactly, but a kind of pressed-brick-and-cement face, a "business" face upon which years and feelings had made no mark—in which cocktails might eventually blast out a few hollows. He had never seen himself so distinctly in his shaving-glass as he did in that instant when Kitty Ayrshire's liquid eye held him, when her bright, inquiring glance roamed over his person. After her prehensile train curled over his boot and she was gone, his wife turned to him and said in the tone of approbation one uses when an infant manifests its groping intelligence, "Very gracious of her, I'm sure!" Mrs. Post nodded oracularly. McKann grunted.

Kitty began her second number, a group of romantic German songs which were altogether more her affair than her first number. When she turned once to acknowledge the applause behind her, she caught McKann in the act of yawning behind his hand—he of course wore no gloves—and he thought she frowned a little. This did not embarrass him; it somehow made him feel important. When she retired after the second part of the program, she again looked him over curiously as she passed, and she took marked precaution that her dress did not touch him. Mrs. Post and his wife again commented upon her consideration.

The final number was made up of modern French songs which Kitty sang enchantingly, and at last her frigid public was thoroughly aroused. While she was coming back again and again to smile and curtsy, McKann whispered to his wife that if there were to be encores he had better make a dash for his train.

"Not at all," put in Mrs. Post. "Kitty is going on the same train. She sings in *Faust* at the opera tomorrow night, so she'll take no chances."

McKann once more told himself how sorry he felt for Post. At last Miss Ayrshire returned, escorted by her accompanist, and gave the people what she of course knew they wanted: the most popular aria from the French opera of which the title-rôle had become synonymous with her name—an opera written for her and to her and round about her, by the veteran French composer who adored her,—the last and not the palest flash of his creative fire. This brought her audience all the way. They clamoured for more of it, but she was not to be coerced. She had been unyielding through storms to which this was a summer breeze. She came on once more, shrugged her shoulders, blew them a kiss, and was gone. Her last smile was for that uncomfortable part of her audience seated behind her, and she looked with recognition at McKann and his ladies as she nodded good night to the wooden chairs.

McKann hurried his charges into the foyer by the nearest exit and put them into his motor. Then he went over to the Schenley to have a glass of beer and a rarebit before train-time. He had not, he admitted to himself, been so much bored as he pretended. The minx herself was well enough, but it was absurd in his fellow-townsmen to look owlish and uplifted about her. He had no rooted dislike for pretty women; he even didn't deny that gay girls had their place in the world, but they ought to be kept in their place. He was born a Presbyterian, just as he was born a McKann. He sat in his pew in the First Church every Sunday, and he never missed a presbytery meeting when he was in town. His religion was not very spiritual, certainly, but it was substantial and concrete, made up of good, hard convictions and opinions. It had something to do with citizenship, with whom one ought to marry, with the coal business (in which his own name was powerful), with the Republican party, and with all majorities and established precedents. He was hostile to fads, to enthusiasms, to individualism, to all changes except in mining machinery and in methods of transportation.

His equanimity restored by his lunch at the Schenley, McKann lit a big cigar, got into his taxi, and bowled off through the sleet.

There was not a sound to be heard or a light to be seen. The ice glittered on the pavement and on the naked trees. No restless feet were abroad. At eleven o'clock the rows of small, comfortable houses looked as empty of the troublesome bubble of life as the Allegheny cemetery itself. Suddenly the cab stopped, and McKann thrust his head out of the window. A woman was standing in the middle of the street addressing his driver in a tone of excitement. Over against the curb a lone electric stood despondent in the storm. The young woman, her cloak blowing about her, turned from the driver to McKann himself, speaking rapidly and somewhat incoherently.

"Could you not be so kind as to help us? It is Mees Ayrshire, the singer. The juice is gone out and we cannot move. We must get to the station. Mademoiselle cannot miss the train; she sings tomorrow night in New York. It is very important. Could you not take us to the station at East Liberty?"

McKann opened the door. "That's all right, but you'll have to hurry. It's eleven-ten now. You've only got fifteen minutes to make the train. Tell her to come along."

The maid drew back and looked up at him in amazement. "But, the hand-luggage to carry, and Mademoiselle to walk! The street is like glass!"

McKann threw away his cigar and followed her. He stood silent by the door of the derelict, while the maid explained that she had found help. The driver had gone off somewhere to telephone for a car. Miss Ayrshire seemed not at all apprehensive; she had not doubted that a rescuer would be forthcoming. She moved deliberately; out of a whirl of skirts she thrust one fur-topped shoe—McKann saw the flash of the gold stocking above it—and alighted.

"So kind of you! So fortunate for us!" she murmured. One hand she placed upon his sleeve, and in the other she carried an armful of roses that had been sent up to the concert stage. The petals showered upon the sooty, sleety pavement as she picked her way along. They would be lying there tomorrow morning, and the children in those houses would wonder if there had been a funeral. The maid followed with two leather bags. As soon as he had lifted Kitty into his cab she exclaimed:

"My jewel-case! I have forgotten it. It is on the back seat, please. I am so careless!"

He dashed back, ran his hand along the cushions, and discovered a small leather bag. When he returned he found the maid and the luggage bestowed on the front seat, and a place left for him on the back seat beside Kitty and her flowers.

"Shall we be taking you far out of your way?" she asked sweetly. "I haven't an idea where the station is. I'm not even sure about the name. Céline thinks it is East Liberty, but I think it is West Liberty. An odd name, anyway. It is a Bohemian quarter, perhaps? A district where the law relaxes a trifle?"

McKann replied grimly that he didn't think the name referred to that kind of liberty.

"So much the better," sighed Kitty. "I am a Californian; that's the only part of America I know very well, and out there, when we called a place Liberty Hill or Liberty Hollow—well, we meant it. You will excuse me if I'm uncommunicative, won't you? I must not talk in this raw air. My throat is sensitive after a long program." She lay back in her corner and closed her eyes.

When the cab rolled down the incline at East Liberty station, the New York express was whistling in. A porter opened the door. McKann sprang out, gave him a claim check and his Pullman ticket, and told him to get his bag at the check-stand and rush it on that train.

Miss Ayrshire, having gathered up her flowers, put out her hand to take his arm. "Why, it's you!" she exclaimed, as she saw his face in the light. "What a coincidence!" She made no further move to alight, but sat smiling as if she had just seated herself in a drawing-room and were ready for talk and a cup of tea.

McKann caught her arm. "You must hurry, Miss Ayrshire, if you mean to catch that train. It stops here only a moment. Can you run?"

"Can I run!" she laughed. "Try me!"

As they raced through the tunnel and up the inside stairway, McKann admitted that he had never before made a dash with feet so quick and sure stepping out beside him. The white-furred boots chased each other like lambs at play, the gold stockings flashed like the spokes of a bicycle wheel in the sun. They reached the door of Miss Ayrshire's state-room just as the train began to pull out. McKann was ashamed of the way he was panting, for Kitty's breathing was as soft and regular as when she was reclining on the back seat of his taxi. It had somehow run in his head that all these stage women were a poor lot physically—unsound, overfed creatures, like canaries that are kept in a cage and stuffed with song-restorer. He retreated to escape her thanks. "Good night! Pleasant journey! Pleasant dreams!" With a friendly nod in Kitty's direction he closed the door behind him.

He was somewhat surprised to find his own bag, his Pullman ticket in the strap, on the seat just outside Kitty's door. But there was nothing strange about it. He had got the last section left on the train, No. 13, next the drawing-room. Every other berth in the car was made up. He was just starting to look for the porter when the door of the state-room opened and Kitty Ayrshire came out. She seated herself carelessly in the front seat beside his bag.

"Please talk to me a little," she said coaxingly. "I'm always wakeful after I sing, and I have to hunt some one to talk to. Céline and I get so tired of each other. We can speak very low, and we shall not disturb any one." She crossed her feet and rested her elbow on his Gladstone. Though she still wore her gold slippers and stockings, she did not, he thanked Heaven, have on her concert gown, but a very demure black velvet with some sort of pearl trimming about the neck. "Wasn't it funny," she proceeded, "that it happened to be you who picked me up? I wanted a word with you, anyway."

McKann smiled in a way that meant he wasn't being taken in. "Did you? We are not very old acquaintances."

"No, perhaps not. But you disapproved tonight, and I thought I was singing very well. You are very critical in such matters?"

He had been standing, but now he sat down. "My dear young lady, I am not critical at all. I know nothing about 'such matters.'"

"And care less?" she said for him, "Well, then we know where we are, in so far as that is concerned. What did displease you? My gown, perhaps? It may seem a little *outré* here, but it's the sort of thing all the imaginative designers abroad are doing. You like the English sort of concert gown better?"

"About gowns," said McKann, "I know even less than about music. If I looked uncomfortable, it was probably because I was uncomfortable. The seats were bad and the lights were annoying."

Kitty looked up with solicitude. "I was sorry they sold those seats. I don't like to make people uncomfortable in any way. Did the lights give you a headache? They are very trying. They burn one's eyes out in the end, I believe." She paused and waved the porter away with a smile as he came toward them. Half-clad Pittsburghers were tramping up and down the aisle, casting sidelong glances at McKann and his companion. "How much better they look with all their clothes on," she murmured. Then, turning directly to McKann again: "I saw you were not well seated, but I felt something quite hostile and personal. You were displeased with me. Doubtless many people are, but I seldom get an opportunity to question them. It would be nice if you took the trouble to tell me why you were displeased."

She spoke frankly, pleasantly, without a shadow of challenge or hauteur. She did not seem to be angling for compliments. McKann settled himself in his seat. He thought he would try her out. She had come for it, and he would let her have it. He found, however, that it was harder to formulate the grounds of his disapproval than he would have supposed. Now that he sat face to face with her, now that she was leaning against his bag, he had no wish to hurt her.

"I'm a hard-headed business man," he said evasively, "and I don't much believe in any of you fluffy-ruffles people. I have a sort of natural distrust of them all, the men more than the women."

She looked thoughtful. "Artists, you mean?" drawing her words slowly. "What is your business?"

"Coal."

"I don't feel any natural distrust of business men, and I know ever so many. I don't know any coal-men, but I think I could become very much interested in coal. Am I larger-minded than you?"

McKann laughed. "I don't think you know when you are interested or when you are not. I don't believe you know what it feels like to be really interested. There is so much fake about your profession. It's an affectation on both sides. I know a great many of the people who went to hear you tonight, and I know that most of them neither know nor care anything about music. They imagine they do, because it's supposed to be the proper thing."

Kitty sat upright and looked interested. She was certainly a lovely creature—the only one of her tribe he had ever seen that he would cross the street to see again. Those were remarkable eyes she had—curious, penetrating, restless, somewhat impudent, but not at all dulled by self-conceit.

"But isn't that so in everything?" she cried. "How many of your clerks are honest because of a fine, individual sense of honour? They are honest because it is the accepted rule of good conduct in business. Do you know"—she looked at him squarely—"I thought you would have something quite definite to say to me; but this is funny-paper stuff, the sort of objection I'd expect from your office-boy."

"Then you don't think it silly for a lot of people to get together and pretend to enjoy something they know nothing about?"

"Of course I think it silly, but that's the way God made audiences. Don't people go to church in exactly the same way? If there were a spiritual-pressure test-machine at the door, I suspect not many of you would get to your pews."

"How do you know I go to church?"

She shrugged her shoulders. "Oh, people with these old, ready-made opinions usually go to church. But you can't evade me like that." She tapped the edge of his seat with the toe of her gold slipper. "You sat there all evening, glaring at me as if you could eat me alive. Now I give you a chance to state your objections, and you merely criticize my audience. What is it? Is it merely that you happen to dislike my personality? In that case, of course, I won't press you."

"No," McKann frowned, "I perhaps dislike your professional personality. As I told you, I have a natural distrust of your variety."

"Natural, I wonder?" Kitty murmured. "I don't see why you should naturally dislike singers any more than I naturally dislike coal-men. I don't classify people by their occupations. Doubtless I should find some coal-men repulsive, and you may find some singers so. But I have reason to believe that, at least, I'm one of the less repellent."

"I don't doubt it," McKann laughed, "and you're a shrewd woman to boot. But you are, all of you, according to my standards, light people. You're brilliant, some of you, but you've no depth."

Kitty seemed to assent, with a dive of her girlish head. "Well, it's a merit in some things to be heavy, and in others to be light. Some things are meant to go deep, and others to go high. Do you want all the women in the world to be profound?"

"You are all," he went on steadily, watching her with indulgence, "fed on hectic emotions. You are pampered. You don't help to carry the burdens of the world. You are self-indulgent and appetent."

"Yes, I am," she assented, with a candour which he did not expect. "Not all artists are, but I am. Why not? If I could once get a convincing statement as to why I should not be self-indulgent, I might change my ways. As for the burdens of the world—" Kitty rested her chin on her clasped hands and looked thoughtful. "One should give pleasure to others. My dear sir, granting that the great majority of people can't enjoy anything very keenly, you'll admit that I give pleasure to many more people than you do. One should help others who are less fortunate; at present I am supporting just eight people, besides those I hire. There was never another family in California that had so many cripples and hard-luckers as that into which I had the honour to be born. The only ones who could take care of themselves were ruined by the San Francisco earthquake some time ago. One should make personal sacrifices. I do; I give money and time and effort to talented students. Oh, I give something much more than that! something that you probably have never given to any one. I give, to the really gifted ones, my *wish*, my desire, my light, if I have any; and that, Mr. Worldly Wiseman, is like giving one's blood! It's the kind of thing you prudent people never give. That is what was in the box of precious ointment." Kitty threw off her fervour with a slight gesture, as if it were a scarf, and leaned back, tucking her slipper up on the edge of his seat. "If you saw the houses I keep up," she sighed, "and the people I employ, and the motor-cars I run—And, after all, I've only this to do it with." She indicated her slender person, which Marshall could almost have broken in two with his bare hands.

She was, he thought, very much like any other charming woman, except that she was more so. Her familiarity was natural and simple. She was at ease because she was not afraid of him or of herself, or of certain half-clad acquaintances of his who had been wandering up and down the car oftener than was necessary. Well, he was not afraid, either.

Kitty put her arms over her head and sighed again, feeling

the smooth part in her black hair. Her head was small—capable of great agitation, like a bird's; or of great resignation, like a nun's. "I can't see why I shouldn't be self-indulgent, when I indulge others. I can't understand your equivocal scheme of ethics. Now I can understand Count Tolstoy's, perfectly. I had a long talk with him once, about his book 'What is Art?' As nearly as I could get it, he believes that we are a race who can exist only by gratifying appetites; the appetites are evil, and the existence they carry on is evil. We were always sad, he says, without knowing why; even in the Stone Age. In some miraculous way a divine ideal was disclosed to us, directly at variance with our appetites. It gave us a new craving, which we could only satisfy by starving all the other hungers in us. Happiness lies in ceasing to be and to cause being, because the thing revealed to us is dearer than any existence our appetites can ever get for us. I can understand that. It's something one often feels in art. It is even the subject of the greatest of all operas, which, because I can never hope to sing it, I love more than all the others." Kitty pulled herself up. "Perhaps you agree with Tolstoy?" she added languidly.

"No; I think he's a crank," said McKann, cheerfully.

"What do you mean by a crank?"

"I mean an extremist."

Kitty laughed. "Weighty word! You'll always have a world full of people who keep to the golden mean. Why bother yourself about me and Tolstoy?"

"I don't, except when you bother me."

"Poor man! It's true this isn't your fault. Still, you did provoke it by glaring at me. Why did you go to the concert?"

"I was dragged."

"I might have known!" she chuckled, and shook her head. "No, you don't give me any good reasons. Your morality seems to me the compromise of cowardice, apologetic and sneaking. When righteousness becomes alive and burning, you hate it as much as you do beauty. You want a little of each in your life, perhaps—adulterated, sterilized, with the sting taken out. It's true enough they are both fearsome things when they get loose in the world; they don't, often."

McKann hated tall talk. "My views on women," he said slowly, "are simple."

"Doubtless," Kitty responded dryly, "but are they consistent? Do you apply them to your stenographers as well as to me? I take it for granted you have unmarried stenographers. Their position, economically, is the same as mine."

McKann studied the toe of her shoe. "With a woman, everything comes back to one thing." His manner was judicial.

She laughed indulgently. "So we are getting down to brass tacks, eh? I have beaten you in argument, and now you are leading trumps."

She put her hands behind her head and her lips parted in a half-yawn. "Does everything come back to one thing? I wish I knew! It's more than likely that, under the same conditions, I should have been very like your stenographers—if they are good ones. Whatever I was, I would have been a good one. I think people are very much alike. You are more different than any one I have met for some time, but I know that there are a great many more at home like you. And even you—I believe there is a real creature down under these custom-made prejudices that save you the trouble of thinking. If you and I were shipwrecked on a desert island, I have no doubt that we would come to a simple and natural understanding. I'm neither a coward nor a shirk. You would find, if you had to undertake any enterprise of danger or difficulty with a woman, that there are several qualifications quite as important as the one to which you doubtless refer."

McKann felt nervously for his watch-chain. "Of course," he brought out, "I am not laying down any generalizations—" His brows wrinkled.

"Oh, aren't you?" murmured Kitty. "Then I totally misunderstood. But remember"—holding up a finger—"It is you, not I, who are afraid to pursue this subject further. Now, I'll tell you something." She leaned forward and clasped her slim, white hands about her velvet knee. "I am as much a victim of these ineradicable prejudices as you. Your stenographer seems to you a better sort. Well, she does to me. Just because her life is, presumably, greyer than mine, she seems better. My mind tells me that dulness, and a mediocre order of ability, and poverty, are not in themselves admirable things. Yet in my heart I always feel that the sales-women in shops and the working girls in factories are more meritorious than I. Many of them, with my opportunities, would be more selfish than I am. Some of them, with their own opportunities, are more selfish. Yet I make this sentimental genuflection before the nun and the charwoman. Tell me, haven't you any weakness? Isn't there any foolish natural thing that unbends you a trifle and makes you feel gay?"

"I like to go fishing."

"To see how many fish you can catch?"

"No, I like the woods and the weather. I like to play a fish and work hard for him. I like the pussy-willows and the cold; and the sky, whether it's blue or grey—night coming on, every thing about it."

He spoke devoutly, and Kitty watched him through half-closed eyes. "And you like to feel that there are light-minded girls like me, who only care about the inside of shops and theatres and hotels, eh? You amuse me, you and your fish! But I mustn't keep you any longer. Haven't I given you every opportunity to state your case against me? I thought you would have more to say for yourself. Do you know, I believe it's not a case you have at all, but a grudge. I believe you are envious; that you'd like to be a tenor, and a perfect lady-killer!" She rose, smiling, and paused with her hand on the door of her stateroom. "Anyhow, thank you for a pleasant evening. And, by the way, dream of me tonight, and not of either of those ladies who sat beside you. It does not matter much whom we live with in this world, but it matters a great deal whom we dream of." She noticed his bricky flush. "You are very naive, after all, but, oh, so cautious! You are naturally afraid of everything new, just as I naturally want to try everything: new people, new religions—new miseries, even. If only there were more new things—If only you were really new! I might learn something. I'm like the Queen of Sheba—I'm not above learning. But you, my friend, would be afraid to try a new shaving soap. It isn't gravitation that holds the world in place; it's the lazy, obese cowardice of the people on it. All the same"— taking his hand and smiling encouragingly—"I'm going to haunt you a little. *Adios!*"

When Kitty entered her state-room, Céline, in her dressing-gown, was nodding by the window.

"Mademoiselle found the fat gentleman interesting?" she asked. "It is nearly one."

"Negatively interesting. His kind always say the same thing. If I could find one really intelligent man who held his views, I should adopt them."

"Monsieur did not look like an original," murmured Céline, as she began to take down her lady's hair.

McKann slept heavily, as usual, and the porter had to shake him in the morning. He sat up in his berth, and, after composing his hair with his fingers, began to hunt about for his clothes. As he put up the window-blind some bright object in the little hammock over his bed caught the sunlight and glittered. He stared and picked up a delicately turned gold slipper.

"Minx! hussy!" he ejaculated. "All that tall talk—! Probably got it from some man who hangs about; learned it off like a parrot. Did she poke this in here herself last night, or did she send that sneak-faced Frenchwoman? I like her nerve!" He wondered whether he might have been breathing audibly when the intruder thrust her head between his curtains. He was conscious that he did not look a Prince Charming in his sleep. He dressed as fast as he could, and, when he was ready to go to the wash-room, glared at the slipper. If the porter should start to make up his berth in his absence—He caught the slipper, wrapped it in his pajama jacket, and thrust it into his bag. He escaped from the train without seeing his tormentor again.

Later McKann threw the slipper into the waste-basket in his room at the Knickerbocker, but the chambermaid, seeing that it was new and mateless, thought there must be a mistake, and placed it in his clothes-closet. He found it there when he returned from the theatre that evening. Considerably mellowed by food and drink and cheerful company, he took the slipper in his hand and decided to keep it as a reminder that absurd things could happen to people of the most clocklike deportment. When he got back to Pittsburgh, he stuck it in a lock-box in his vault, safe from prying clerks.

McKann has been ill for five years now, poor fellow! He still goes to the office, because it is the only place that interests him, but his partners do most of the work, and his clerks find him sadly changed—"Morbid," they call his state of mind. He has had the pine-trees in his yard cut down because they remind him of cemeteries. On Sundays or holidays, when the office is empty, and he takes his will or his insurance-policies out of his lock-box, he often puts the tarnished gold slipper on his desk and looks at it. Somehow it suggests life to his tired mind, as his pine-trees suggested death—life and youth. When he drops over some day, his executors will be puzzled by the slipper.

As for Kitty Ayrshire, she has played so many jokes, practical and impractical, since then, that she has long ago forgotten the night when she threw away a slipper to be a thorn in the side of a just man.

Louisa May Alcott

L ouisa May Alcott was the hero of her own story.

At first, she wrote herself and her sisters into stories and plays where they were knights and princes and villains, sometimes damsels, occasionally in distress, but they were stories of action where the girls were empowered to make choices, take up swords, and save themselves. Yet the real heroism was in Alcott's act of writing. She gave herself and her sisters respites from the hardship of poverty—not the charming penny-pinching of *Little Women* where there wasn't always enough money for limes or a new dress, but an abject, cold-and-hungry poverty. She gave them a sense of agency in the years when, as children (along with their mother), they had no choice but to follow their father, Bronson Alcott, who was loving but neglectful to the point of abuse. He led them from one failed experiment to another, in a steady decline, until the disaster of his utopian community, Fruitlands, nearly killed them all, and their mother, Abba Alcott, had had enough and took them all back to Concord.

By age fifteen, bitterly aware that her father either wouldn't or couldn't do anything to support the family, Alcott turned to teaching, domestic work, and nearly anything else that would make money so she could rescue her mother and sisters from the quicksand of poverty. She continued to write, perhaps to save her spirit in the face of draining, daily service that paid a mere pittance. She wrote the stories she wanted to read—thrillers with bold female characters transcending gender restrictions and shaping their own destinies. The women were sometimes virtuous and sometimes villainous, but they were always victorious. And so was Alcott when she started selling her sensational stories under the genderless pseudonym a.m. Barnard and was soon making enough money to stop her other work.

Sadly, the best heroes are often asked to make sacrifices for the greater good. Jo cuts off her beautiful hair so Marmee has the money to travel to their sick father, and Alcott gives up her "blood and thunder" thrillers to write *Little Women* because her publisher asks for it. She didn't want to write it, as she confesses in her journal, "Mr. N wants a girls' story, and I begin 'Little Women.' I plod away, though I don't enjoy this sort of thing." She tells a fan that she wrote the book (and its sequels) because they paid well. In a letter to her niece years later, Alcott writes, "Freedom has always been my longing, but I have never had it." In order to save her family, Alcott sacrificed the freedom to follow her own muse, and again, our hero emerges victorious. *Little Women* and its sequels provide financial security for herself and her family for generations.

But Louisa May Alcott's legacy isn't measured in books sold or money made. Her sacrifice has served the greater good in ways she could have never imagined. In this book that she reluctantly wrote and yet still invested with herself and soul, she gives us the character, Jo March, who has inspired countless women writers for 150 years to pick up their pens, to write about their own lives, complex and courageous, with the same gravitas as men. Alcott calls us all to claim our own agency, empowering us to save ourselves.

And that makes her the hero of our story too.

LILY-BELL AND
THISTLEDOWN

O nce upon a time, two little Fairies went out into the world, to seek their fortune. Thistledown was as gay and gallant a little Elf as ever spread a wing. His purple mantle, and doublet of green, were embroidered with the brightest threads, and the plume in his cap came always from the wing of the gayest butterfly.

But he was not loved in Fairy-Land, for, like the flower whose name and colors he wore, though fair to look upon, many were the little thorns of cruelty and selfishness that lay concealed by his gay mantle. Many a gentle flower and harmless bird died by his hand, for he cared for himself alone, and whatever gave him pleasure must be his, though happy hearts were rendered sad, and peaceful homes destroyed.

Such was Thistledown; but far different was his little friend, Lily-Bell. Kind, compassionate, and loving, wherever her gentle face was seen, joy and gratitude were found; no suffering flower or insect, that did not love and bless the kindly Fairy; and thus all Elf-Land looked upon her as a friend.

Nor did this make her vain and heedless of others; she humbly dwelt among them, seeking to do all the good she might; and many a houseless bird and hungry insect that Thistledown had harmed did she feed and shelter, and in return no evil could befall her, for so many friends were all about her, seeking to repay her tenderness and love by their watchful care.

She would not now have left Fairy-Land, but to help and counsel her wild companion, Thistledown, who, discontented with his quiet home, WOULD seek his fortune in the great world, and she feared he would suffer from his own faults for others would not always be as gentle and forgiving as his kindred. So the kind little Fairy left her home and friends to go with him; and thus, side by side, they flew beneath the bright summer sky.

On and on, over hill and valley, they went, chasing the gay butterflies, or listening to the bees, as they flew from flower to flower like busy little housewives, singing as they worked; till at last they reached a pleasant garden, filled with flowers and green, old trees.

"See," cried Thistledown, "what a lovely home is here; let us rest among the cool leaves, and hear the flowers sing, for I am sadly tired and hungry."

So into the quiet garden they went, and the winds gayly welcomed them, while the flowers nodded on their stems, offering their bright leaves for the Elves to rest upon, and fresh, sweet honey to refresh them.

"Now, dear Thistle, do not harm these friendly blossoms," said Lily-Bell; "see how kindly they spread their leaves, and offer us their dew. It would be very wrong in you to repay their care with cruelty and pain. You will be tender for my sake, dear Thistle."

Then she went among the flowers, and they bent lovingly before her, and laid their soft leaves against her little face, that she might see how glad they were to welcome one so good and gentle, and kindly offered their dew and honey to the weary little Fairy, who sat among their fragrant petals and looked smilingly on the happy blossoms, who, with their soft, low voices, sang her to sleep.

While Lily-Bell lay dreaming among the rose-leaves, Thistledown went wandering through the garden. First he robbed the bees of their honey, and rudely shook the little flowers, that he might get the dew they had gathered to bathe their buds in. Then he chased the bright winged flies, and wounded them with the sharp thorn he carried for a sword; he broke the spider's shining webs, lamed the birds, and soon wherever he passed lay wounded insects and drooping flowers; while the winds carried the tidings over the garden, and bird and blossom looked upon him as an evil spirit, and fled away or closed their leaves, lest he should harm them.

Thus he went, leaving sorrow and pain behind him, till he

came to the roses where Lily-Bell lay sleeping. There, weary of his cruel sport, he stayed to rest beneath a graceful rose-tree, where grew one blooming flower and a tiny bud.

"Why are you so slow in blooming, little one? You are too old to be rocked in your green cradle longer, and should be out among your sister flowers," said Thistle, as he lay idly in the shadow of the tree.

"My little bud is not yet strong enough to venture forth," replied the rose, as she bent fondly over it; "the sunlight and the rain would blight her tender form, were she to blossom now, but soon she will be fit to bear them; till then she is content to rest beside her mother, and to wait."

"You silly flower," said Thistledown, "see how quickly I will make you bloom! your waiting is all useless." And speaking thus, he pulled rudely apart the folded leaves, and laid them open to the sun and air; while the rose mother implored the cruel Fairy to leave her little bud untouched.

"It is my first, my only one," said she, "and I have watched over it with such care, hoping it would soon bloom beside me; and now you have destroyed it. How could you harm the little helpless one, that never did aught to injure you?" And while her tears fell like summer rain, she drooped in grief above the little bud, and sadly watched it fading in the sunlight; but Thistledown, heedless of the sorrow he had given, spread his wings and flew away.

Soon the sky grew dark, and heavy drops began to fall. Then Thistle hastened to the lily, for her cup was deep, and the white leaves fell like curtains over the fragrant bed; he was a dainty little Elf, and could not sleep among the clovers and bright buttercups. But when he asked the flower to unfold her leaves and take him in, she turned her pale, soft face away, and answered sadly, "I must shield my little drooping sisters whom you have harmed, and cannot let you in."

Then Thistledown was very angry, and turned to find shelter among the stately roses; but they showed their sharp thorns, and, while their rosy faces glowed with anger, told him to begone, or they would repay him for the wrong he had done their gentle kindred.

He would have stayed to harm them, but the rain fell fast, and he hurried away, saying, "The tulips will take me in, for I have praised their beauty, and they are vain and foolish flowers."

But when he came, all wet and cold, praying for shelter among their thick leaves, they only laughed and said scornfully, "We know you, and will not let you in, for you are false and cruel, and will only bring us sorrow. You need not come to us for another mantle, when the rain has spoilt your fine one; and do not stay here, or we will do you harm."

Then they waved their broad leaves stormily, and scattered the heavy drops on his dripping garments.

"Now must I go to the humble daisies and blue violets," said Thistle, "they will be glad to let in so fine a Fairy, and I shall die in this cold wind and rain."

So away he flew, as fast as his heavy wings would bear him,

to the daisies; but they nodded their heads wisely, and closed their leaves yet closer, saying sharply,—

"Go away with yourself, and do not imagine we will open our leaves to you, and spoil our seeds by letting in the rain. It serves you rightly; to gain our love and confidence, and repay it by such cruelty! You will find no shelter here for one whose careless hand wounded our little friend Violet, and broke the truest heart that ever beat in a flower's breast. We are very angry with you, wicked Fairy; go away and hide yourself."

"Ah," cried the shivering Elf, "where can I find shelter? I will go to the violets: they will forgive and take me in."

But the daisies had spoken truly; the gentle little flower was dead, and her blue-eyed sisters were weeping bitterly over her faded leaves.

"Now I have no friends," sighed poor Thistledown, "and must die of cold. Ah, if I had but minded Lily-Bell, I might now be dreaming beneath some flower's leaves."

"Others can forgive and love, beside Lily-Bell and Violet," said a faint, sweet voice; "I have no little bud to shelter now, and you can enter here." It was the rose mother that spoke, and Thistle saw how pale the bright leaves had grown, and how the slender stem was bowed. Grieved, ashamed, and wondering at the flower's forgiving words, he laid his weary head on the bosom he had filled with sorrow, and the fragrant leaves were folded carefully about him.

But he could find no rest. The rose strove to comfort him;

but when she fancied he was sleeping, thoughts of her lost bud stole in, and the little heart beat so sadly where he lay, that no sleep came; while the bitter tears he had caused to flow fell more coldly on him than the rain without. Then he heard the other flowers whispering among themselves of his cruelty, and the sorrow he had brought to their happy home; and many wondered how the rose, who had suffered most, could yet forgive and shelter him.

"Never could I forgive one who had robbed me of my children. I could bow my head and die, but could give no happiness to one who had taken all my own," said Hyacinth, bending fondly over the little ones that blossomed by her side.

"Dear Violet is not the only one who will leave us," sobbed little Mignonette; "the rose mother will fade like her little bud, and we shall lose our gentlest teacher. Her last lesson is forgiveness; let us show our love for her, and the gentle stranger Lily-Bell, by allowing no unkind word or thought of him who has brought us all this grief."

The angry words were hushed, and through the long night nothing was heard but the dropping of the rain, and the low sighs of the rose.

Soon the sunlight came again, and with it Lily-Bell seeking for Thistledown; but he was ashamed, and stole away.

When the flowers told their sorrow to kind-hearted Lily-Bell, she wept bitterly at the pain her friend had given, and with loving words strove to comfort those whom he had grieved; with gentle care she healed the wounded birds, and watched above the flowers he had harmed, bringing each day dew and sunlight to refresh and strengthen, till all were well again; and though sorrowing for their dead friends, still they forgave Thistle for the sake of her who had done so much for them. Thus, erelong, buds fairer than that she had lost lay on the rose mother's breast, and for all she had suffered she was well repaid by the love of Lily-Bell and her sister flowers.

And when bird, bee, and blossom were strong and fair again, the gentle Fairy said farewell, and flew away to seek her friend, leaving behind many grateful hearts, who owed their joy and life to her.

Meanwhile, over hill and dale went Thistledown, and for a time was kind and gentle to every living thing. He missed sadly the little friend who had left her happy home to watch over him, but he was too proud to own his fault, and so went on, hoping she would find him.

One day he fell asleep, and when he woke the sun had set, and the dew began to fall; the flower-cups were closed, and he had nowhere to go, till a friendly little bee, belated by his heavy load of honey, bid the weary Fairy come with him.

"Help me to bear my honey home, and you can stay with us tonight," he kindly said.

So Thistle gladly went with him, and soon they came to a pleasant garden, where among the fairest flowers stood the hive, covered with vines and overhung with blossoming trees.

Glow-worms stood at the door to light them home, and as they passed in, the Fairy thought how charming it must be to dwell in such a lovely place. The floor of wax was pure and white as marble, while the walls were formed of golden honey-comb, and the air was fragrant with the breath of flowers.

"You cannot see our Queen to-night," said the little bee, "but I will show you to a bed where you can rest."

And he led the tired Fairy to a little cell, where on a bed of flower-leaves he folded his wings and fell asleep.

As the first ray of sunlight stole in, he was awakened by sweet music. It was the morning song of the bees.

> "Awake! awake! for the earliest gleam
> Of golden sunlight shines
> On the rippling waves, that brightly flow
> Beneath the flowering vines.
> Awake! awake! for the low, sweet chant
> Of the wild-birds' morning hymn
> Comes floating by on the fragrant air,
> Through the forest cool and dim;
> Then spread each wing,
> And work, and sing,
> Through the long, bright sunny hours;
> O'er the pleasant earth
> We journey forth,
> For a day among the flowers.

"Awake! awake! for the summer wind
Hath bidden the blossoms unclose,
Hath opened the violet's soft blue eye,
And wakened the sleeping rose.
And lightly they wave on their slender stems
Fragrant, and fresh, and fair,
Waiting for us, as we singing come
To gather our honey-dew there.
Then spread each wing,
And work, and sing,
Through the long, bright sunny hours;
O'er the pleasant earth
We journey forth,
For a day among the flowers!"

Soon his friend came to bid him rise, as the Queen desired to speak with him. So, with his purple mantle thrown gracefully over his shoulder, and his little cap held respectfully in his hand, he followed Nimble-Wing to the great hall, where the Queen was being served by her little pages. Some bore her fresh dew and honey, some fanned her with fragrant flower-leaves, while others scattered the sweetest perfumes on the air.

"Little Fairy," said the Queen, "you are welcome to my palace; and we will gladly have you stay with us, if you will obey our laws. We do not spend the pleasant summer days in idleness and pleasure, but each one labors for the happiness and good of all. If our home is beautiful, we have made it so by industry; and here, as one large, loving family, we dwell; no sorrow, care, or discord can enter in, while all obey the voice of her who seeks to be a wise and gentle Queen to them. If you will stay with us, we will teach you many things. Order, patience, industry, who can teach so well as they who are the emblems of these virtues?

"Our laws are few and simple. You must each day gather your share of honey, see that your cell is sweet and fresh, as you yourself must be; rise with the sun, and with him to sleep. You must harm no flower in doing your work, nor take more than your just share of honey; for they so kindly give us food, it were most cruel to treat them with aught save gentleness and gratitude. Now will you stay with us, and learn what even mortals seek to know, that labor brings true happiness?"

And Thistle said he would stay and dwell with them; for he was tired of wandering alone, and thought he might live here till Lily-Bell should come, or till he was weary of the kind-hearted bees. Then they took away his gay garments, and dressed him like themselves, in the black velvet cloak with golden bands across his breast.

"Now come with us," they said. So forth into the green fields they went, and made their breakfast among the dewy flowers; and then till the sun set they flew from bud to blossom, singing as they went; and Thistle for a while was happier than when breaking flowers and harming gentle birds.

But he soon grew tired of working all day in the sun, and

longed to be free again. He could find no pleasure with the industrious bees, and sighed to be away with his idle friends, the butterflies; so while the others worked he slept or played, and then, in haste to get his share, he tore the flowers, and took all they had saved for their own food. Nor was this all; he told such pleasant tales of the life he led before he came to live with them, that many grew unhappy and discontented, and they who had before wished no greater joy than the love and praise of their kind Queen, now disobeyed and blamed her for all she had done for them.

Long she bore with their unkind words and deeds; and when at length she found it was the ungrateful Fairy who had wrought this trouble in her quiet kingdom, she strove, with sweet, forgiving words, to show him all the wrong he had done; but he would not listen, and still went on destroying the happiness of those who had done so much for him.

Then, when she saw that no kindness could touch his heart, she said:—

"Thistledown, we took you in, a friendless stranger, fed and clothed you, and made our home as pleasant to you as we could; and in return for all our care, you have brought discontent and trouble to my subjects, grief and care to me. I cannot let my peaceful kingdom be disturbed by you; therefore go and seek another home. You may find other friends, but none will love you more than we, had you been worthy of it; so farewell." And the doors of the once happy home he had disturbed were closed behind him.

Then he was very angry, and determined to bring some great sorrow on the good Queen. So he sought out the idle, wilful bees, whom he had first made discontented, bidding them follow him, and win the honey the Queen had stored up for the winter.

"Let us feast and make merry in the pleasant summer-time," said Thistle; "winter is far off, why should we waste these lovely days, toiling to lay up the food we might enjoy now. Come, we will take what we have made, and think no more of what the Queen has said."

So while the industrious bees were out among the flow-ers, he led the drones to the hive, and took possession of the honey, destroying and laying waste the home of the kind bees; then, fearing that in their grief and anger they might harm him, Thistle flew away to seek new friends.

After many wanderings, he came at length to a great forest, and here beside a still lake he stayed to rest. Delicate wood-flowers grew near him in the deep green moss, with drooping heads, as if they listened to the soft wind singing among the pines. Bright-eyed birds peeped at him from their nests, and many-colored insects danced above the cool, still lake.

"This is a pleasant place," said Thistle; "it shall be my home for a while. Come hither, blue dragon-fly, I would gladly make a friend of you, for I am all alone."

The dragon-fly folded his shining wings beside the Elf, lis-tened to the tale he told, promised to befriend the lonely one, and strove to make the forest a happy home to him.

So here dwelt Thistle, and many kind friends gathered round him, for he spoke gently to them, and they knew nothing of the cruel deeds he had done; and for a while he was happy and content. But at length he grew weary of the gentle birds, and wild-flowers, and sought new pleasure in destroying the beauty he was tired of; and soon the friends who had so kindly welcomed him looked upon him as an evil spirit, and shrunk away as he approached.

At length his friend the dragon-fly besought him to leave the quiet home he had disturbed. Then Thistle was very angry, and while the dragon-fly was sleeping among the flowers that hung over the lake, he led an ugly spider to the spot, and bade him weave his nets about the sleeping insect, and bind him fast. The cruel spider gladly obeyed the ungrateful Fairy; and soon the poor fly could move neither leg nor wing. Then Thistle flew away through the wood, leaving sorrow and trouble behind him.

He had not journeyed far before he grew weary, and lay down to rest. Long he slept, and when he awoke, and tried to rise, his hands and wings were bound; while beside him stood two strange little figures, with dark faces and garments, that rustled like withered leaves; who cried to him, as he struggled to get free,—

"Lie still, you naughty Fairy, you are in the Brownies' power, and shall be well punished for your cruelty ere we let you go."

So poor Thistle lay sorrowfully, wondering what would come of it, and wishing Lily-Bell would come to help and comfort him; but he had left her, and she could not help him now.

Soon a troop of Brownies came rustling through the air, and

gathered round him, while one who wore an acorn-cup on his head, and was their King, said, as he stood beside the trembling Fairy,—

"You have done many cruel things, and caused much sorrow to happy hearts; now you are in my power, and I shall keep you prisoner till you have repented. You cannot dwell on the earth without harming the fair things given you to enjoy, so you shall live alone in solitude and darkness, till you have learned to find happiness in gentle deeds, and forget yourself in giving joy to others. When you have learned this, I will set you free."

Then the Brownies bore him to a high, dark rock, and, entering a little door, led him to a small cell, dimly lighted by a crevice through which came a single gleam of sunlight; and there, through long, long days, poor Thistle sat alone, and gazed with wistful eyes at the little opening, longing to be out on the green earth. No one came to him, but the silent Brownies who brought his daily food; and with bitter tears he wept for Lily-Bell, mourning his cruelty and selfishness, seeking to do some kindly deed that might atone for his wrong-doing.

A little vine that grew outside his prison rock came creeping up, and looked in through the crevice, as if to cheer the lonely Fairy, who welcomed it most gladly, and daily sprinkled its soft leaves with his small share of water, that the little vine might live, even if it darkened more and more his dim cell.

The watchful Brownies saw this kind deed, and brought him fresh flowers, and many things, which Thistle gratefully received, though he never knew it was his kindness to the vine that gained for him these pleasures.

Thus did poor Thistle strive to be more gentle and unselfish, and grew daily happier and better.

Now while Thistledown was a captive in the lonely cell, Lily-Bell was seeking him far and wide, and sadly traced him by the sorrowing hearts he had left behind.

She healed the drooping flowers, cheered the Queen Bee's grief, brought back her discontented subjects, restored the home to peace and order, and left them blessing her.

Thus she journeyed on, till she reached the forest where Thistledown had lost his freedom. She unbound the starving dragon-fly, and tended the wounded birds; but though all learned to love her, none could tell where the Brownies had borne her friend, till a little wind came whispering by, and told her that a sweet voice had been heard, singing Fairy songs, deep in a moss-grown rock.

Then Lily-Bell went seeking through the forest, listening for the voice. Long she looked and listened in vain; when one day, as she was wandering through a lonely dell, she heard a faint, low sound of music, and soon a distant voice mournfully singing,—

"Bright shines the summer sun,
　Soft is the summer air;
Gayly the wood-birds sing,
　Flowers are blooming fair.

"But, deep in the dark, cold rock,
 Sadly I dwell,
Longing for thee, dear friend,
 Lily-Bell! Lily-Bell!"

"Thistle, dear Thistle, where are you?" joyfully cried Lily-Bell, as she flew from rock to rock. But the voice was still, and she would have looked in vain, had she not seen a little vine, whose green leaves fluttering to and fro seemed beckoning her to come; and as she stood among its flowers she sang,—

"Through sunlight and summer air
 I have sought for thee long,
Guided by birds and flowers,
 And now by thy song.

"Thistledown! Thistledown!
 O'er hill and dell
Hither to comfort thee
 Comes Lily-Bell."

Then from the vine-leaves two little arms were stretched out to her, and Thistledown was found. So Lily-Bell made her home in the shadow of the vine, and brought such joy to Thistle, that his lonely cell seemed pleasanter to him than all the world beside; and he grew daily more like his gentle friend. But it did not last long, for one day she did not come. He watched and waited long, for the little face that used to peep smiling in through the vine-leaves. He called and beckoned through the narrow opening, but no Lily-Bell answered; and he wept sadly as he thought of all she had done for him, and that now he could not go to seek and help her, for he had lost his freedom by his own cruel and wicked deeds.

At last he besought the silent Brownie earnestly to tell him whither she had gone.

"O let me go to her," prayed Thistle; "if she is in sorrow, I will comfort her, and show my gratitude for all she has done for me: dear Brownie, set me free, and when she is found I will come and be your prisoner again. I will bear and suffer any danger for her sake."

"Lily-Bell is safe," replied the Brownie; "come, you shall learn the trial that awaits you."

Then he led the wondering Fairy from his prison, to a group of tall, drooping ferns, beneath whose shade a large white lily had been placed, forming a little tent, within which, on a couch of thick green moss, lay Lily-Bell in a deep sleep; the sunlight stole softly in, and all was cool and still.

"You cannot wake her," said the Brownie, as Thistle folded his arms tenderly about her. "It is a magic slumber, and she will not wake till you shall bring hither gifts from the Earth, Air, and Water Spirits. 'T is a long and weary task, for you have made no friends to help you, and will have to seek for them

alone. This is the trial we shall give you; and if your love for
Lily-Bell be strong enough to keep you from all cruelty and
selfishness, and make you kind and loving as you should be,
she will awake to welcome you, and love you still more fondly
than before."

Then Thistle, with a last look on the little friend he loved so
well, set forth alone to his long task.

The home of the Earth Spirits was the first to find, and no
one would tell him where to look. So far and wide he wandered,
through gloomy forests and among lonely hills, with none to
cheer him when sad and weary, none to guide him on his way.

On he went, thinking of Lily-Bell, and for her sake bear-
ing all; for in his quiet prison many gentle feelings and kindly
thoughts had sprung up in his heart, and he now strove to be
friends with all, and win for himself the love and confidence of
those whom once he sought to harm and cruelly destroy.

But few believed him; for they remembered his false prom-
ises and evil deeds, and would not trust him now; so poor Thistle
found few to love or care for him.

Long he wandered, and carefully he sought; but could not
find the Earth Spirits' home. And when at length he reached
the pleasant garden where he and Lily-Bell first parted, he said
within himself,—

"Here I will stay awhile, and try to win by kindly deeds the
flowers' forgiveness for the pain and sorrow I brought them long
ago; and they may learn to love and trust me. So, even if I never

find the Spirits, I shall be worthier Lily-Bell's affection if I strive to atone for the wrong I have done."

Then he went among the flowers, but they closed their leaves, and shrank away, trembling with fear; while the birds fled to hide among the leaves as he passed.

This grieved poor Thistle, and he longed to tell them how changed he had become; but they would not listen. So he tried to show, by quiet deeds of kindness, that he meant no harm to them; and soon the kind-hearted birds pitied the lonely Fairy, and when he came near sang cheering songs, and dropped ripe berries in his path, for he no longer broke their eggs, or hurt their little ones.

And when the flowers saw this, and found the once cruel Elf now watering and tending little buds, feeding hungry insects, and helping the busy ants to bear their heavy loads, they shared the pity of the birds, and longed to trust him; but they dared not yet.

He came one day, while wandering through the garden, to the little rose he had once harmed so sadly. Many buds now bloomed beside her, and her soft face glowed with motherly pride, as she bent fondly over them. But when Thistle came, he saw with sorrow how she bade them close their green curtains, and conceal themselves beneath the leaves, for there was danger near; and, drooping still more closely over them, she seemed to wait with trembling fear the cruel Fairy's coming.

But no rude hand tore her little ones away, no unkind words were spoken; but a soft shower of dew fell lightly on them, and Thistle, bending tenderly above them, said,—

"Dear flower, forgive the sorrow I once brought you, and trust me now for Lily-Bell's sake. Her gentleness has changed my cruelty to kindness, and I would gladly repay all for the harm I have done; but none will love and trust me now."

Then the little rose looked up, and while the dew-drops shone like happy tears upon her leaves, she said,—

"I WILL love and trust you, Thistle, for you are indeed much changed. Make your home among us, and my sister flowers will soon learn to love you as you deserve. Not for sweet Lily-Bell's sake, but for your own, will I become your friend; for you are kind and gentle now, and worthy of our love. Look up, my little ones, there is no danger near; look up, and welcome Thistle to our home."

Then the little buds raised their rosy faces, danced again upon their stems, and nodded kindly at Thistle, who smiled on them through happy tears, and kissed the sweet, forgiving rose, who loved and trusted him when most forlorn and friendless.

But the other flowers wondered among themselves, and Hyacinth said,—

"If Rose-Leaf is his friend, surely we may be; yet still I fear he may soon grow weary of this gentleness, and be again the wicked Fairy he once was, and we shall suffer for our kindness to him now."

"Ah, do not doubt him!" cried warm-hearted little Mignonette; "surely some good spirit has changed the wicked Thistle into this good little Elf. See how tenderly he lifts aside the leaves that overshadow pale Harebell, and listen now how softly he sings as he rocks little Eglantine to sleep. He has done many friendly things, though none save Rose-Leaf has been kind to him, and he is very sad. Last night when I awoke to draw my curtains closer, he sat weeping in the moonlight, so bitterly, I longed to speak a kindly word to him. Dear sisters, let us trust him."

And they all said little Mignonette was right; and, spreading wide their leaves, they bade him come, and drink their dew, and lie among the fragrant petals, striving to cheer his sorrow. Thistle told them all, and, after much whispering together, they said,—

"Yes, we will help you to find the Earth Spirits, for you are striving to be good, and for love of Lily-Bell we will do much for you."

So they called a little bright-eyed mole, and said, "Downy-Back, we have given you a pleasant home among our roots, and you are a grateful little friend; so will you guide dear Thistle to the Earth Spirits' home?"

Downy-Back said, "Yes," and Thistle, thanking the kindly flowers, followed his little guide, through long, dark galleries, deeper and deeper into the ground; while a glow-worm flew before to light the way. On they went, and after a while, reached a path lit up by bright jewels hung upon the walls. Here Downy-Back, and Glimmer, the glow-worm, left him, saying,—

"We can lead you no farther; you must now go on alone, and the music of the Spirits will guide you to their home."

Then they went quickly up the winding path, and Thistle, guided by the sweet music, went on alone.

He soon reached a lovely spot, whose golden halls were bright with jewels, which sparkled brightly, and threw many-colored shadows on the shining garments of the little Spirits, who danced below to the melody of soft, silvery bells.

Long Thistle stood watching the brilliant forms that flashed and sparkled round him; but he missed the flowers and the sunlight, and rejoiced that he was not an Earth Spirit.

At last they spied him out, and, gladly welcoming him, bade him join in their dance. But Thistledown was too sad for that, and when he told them all his story they no longer urged, but sought to comfort him; and one whom they called little Sparkle (for her crown and robe shone with the brightest diamonds), said: "You will have to work for us, ere you can win a gift to show the Brownies; do you see those golden bells that make such music, as we wave them to and fro? We worked long and hard ere they were won, and you can win one of those, if you will do the task we give you."

And Thistle said, "No task will be too hard for me to do for dear Lily-Bell's sake."

Then they led him to a strange, dark place, lit up with torches; where troops of Spirits flew busily to and fro, among damp rocks, and through dark galleries that led far down into the earth. "What do they here?" asked Thistle.

"I will tell," replied little Sparkle, "for I once worked here myself. Some of them watch above the flower-roots, and keep them fresh and strong; others gather the clear drops that trickle from the damp rocks, and form a little spring, which, growing ever larger, rises to the light above, and gushes forth in some green field or lonely forest; where the wild-birds come to drink, and wood-flowers spread their thirsty leaves above the clear, cool waves, as they go dancing away, carrying joy and freshness wherever they go. Others shape the bright jewels into lovely forms, and make the good-luck pennies which we give to mortals whom we love. And here you must toil till the golden flower is won."

Then Thistle went among the Spirits, and joined in their tasks; he tended the flower-roots, gathered the water-drops, and formed the good-luck pennies. Long and hard he worked, and was often sad and weary, often tempted by unkind and selfish thoughts; but he thought of Lily-Bell, and strove to be kind and loving as she had been; and soon the Spirits learned to love the patient Fairy, who had left his home to toil among them for the sake of his gentle friend.

At length came little Sparkle to him, saying, "You have done enough; come now, and dance and feast with us, for the golden flower is won."

But Thistle could not stay, for half his task was not yet done; and he longed for sunlight and Lily-Bell. So, taking a kind farewell, he hastened through the torch-lit path up to the light again; and, spreading his wings, flew over hill and dale till he reached the forest where Lily-Bell lay sleeping.

It was early morning, and the rosy light shone brightly through the lily-leaves upon her, as Thistle entered, and laid his first gift at the Brownie King's feet.

"You have done well," said he, "we hear good tidings of you from bird and flower, and you are truly seeking to repair the evil you have done. Take now one look at your little friend, and then go forth to seek from the Air Spirits your second gift."

Then Thistle said farewell again to Lily-Bell, and flew far and wide among the clouds, seeking the Air Spirits; but though he wandered till his weary wings could bear him no longer, it was in vain. So, faint and sad, he lay down to rest on a broad vine-leaf, that fluttered gently in the wind; and as he lay, he saw beneath him the home of the kind bees whom he had so disturbed, and Lily-Bell had helped and comforted.

"I will seek to win their pardon, and show them that I am no longer the cruel Fairy who so harmed them," thought Thistle, "and when they become again my friends, I will ask their help to find the Air Spirits; and if I deserve it, they will gladly aid me on my way."

So he flew down into the field below, and hastened busily from flower to flower, till he had filled a tiny blue-bell with sweet, fresh honey. Then he stole softly to the hive, and, placing it near the door, concealed himself to watch. Soon his friend Nimble-Wing came flying home, and when he spied the little cup, he hummed with joy, and called his companions around him.

"Surely, some good Elf has placed it here for us," said they;

"let us bear it to our Queen; it is so fresh and fragrant it will be a fit gift for her"; and they joyfully took it in, little dreaming who had placed it there.

So each day Thistle filled a flower-cup, and laid it at the door; and each day the bees wondered more and more, for many strange things happened. The field-flowers told of the good spirit who watched above them, and the birds sang of the same kind little Elf bringing soft moss for their nests, and food for their hungry young ones; while all around the hive had grown fairer since the Fairy came.

But the bees never saw him, for he feared he had not yet done enough to win their forgiveness and friendship; so he lived alone among the vines, daily bringing them honey, and doing some kindly action.

At length, as he lay sleeping in a flower-bell, a little bee came wandering by, and knew him for the wicked Thistle; so he called his friends, and, as they flew murmuring around him, he awoke.

"What shall we do to you, naughty Elf?" said they. "You are in our power, and we will sting you if you are not still."

"Let us close the flower-leaves around him and leave him here to starve," cried one, who had not yet forgotten all the sorrow Thistle had caused them long ago.

"No, no, that were very cruel, dear Buzz," said little Hum; "let us take him to our Queen, and she will tell us how to show our anger for the wicked deeds he did. See how bitterly he weeps; be kind to him, he will not harm us more.

"You good little Hum!" cried a kind-hearted robin who had hopped near to listen to the bees. "Dear friends, do you not know that this is the good Fairy who has dwelt so quietly among us, watching over bird and blossom, giving joy to all he helps? It is HE who brings the honey-cup each day to you, and then goes silently away, that you may never know who works so faithfully for you. Be kind to him, for if he has done wrong, he has repented of it, as you may see."

"Can this be naughty Thistle?" said Nimble-Wing.

"Yes, it is I," said Thistle, "but no longer cruel and unkind. I have tried to win your love by patient industry. Ah, trust me now, and you shall see I am not naughty Thistle any more."

Then the wondering bees led him to their Queen, and when he had told his tale, and begged their forgiveness, it was gladly given; and all strove to show him that he was loved and trusted. Then he asked if they could tell him where the Air Spirits dwelt, for he must not forget dear Lily-Bell; and to his great joy the Queen said, "Yes," and bade little Hum guide Thistle to Cloud-Land.

Little Hum joyfully obeyed; and Thistle followed him, as he flew higher and higher among the soft clouds, till in the distance they saw a radiant light.

"There is their home, and I must leave you now, dear Thistle," said the little bee; and, bidding him farewell, he flew singing back; while Thistle, following the light, soon found himself in the Air Spirits' home.

The sky was gold and purple like an autumn sunset, and long walls of brilliant clouds lay round him. A rosy light shone through the silver mist, on gleaming columns and the rainbow roof; soft, fragrant winds went whispering by, and airy little forms were flitting to and fro.

Long Thistle wondered at the beauty round him; and then he went among the shining Spirits, told his tale, and asked a gift.

But they answered like the Earth Spirits. "You must serve us first, and then we will gladly give you a robe of sunlight like our own."

And then they told him how they wafted flower-seeds over the earth, to beautify and brighten lonely spots; how they watched above the blossoms by day, and scattered dews at night, brought sunlight into darkened places, and soft winds to refresh and cheer.

"These are the things we do," said they, " and you must aid us for a time."

And Thistle gladly went with the lovely Spirits; by day he joined the sunlight and the breeze in their silent work; by night, with Star-Light and her sister spirits, he flew over the moon-lit earth, dropping cool dew upon the folded flowers, and bringing happy dreams to sleeping mortals. Many a kind deed was done, many a gentle word was spoken; and each day lighter grew his heart, and stronger his power of giving joy to others.

At length Star-Light bade him work no more, and gladly gave him the gift he had won. Then his second task was done, and he flew gayly back to the green earth and slumbering Lily-Bell.

The silvery moonlight shone upon her, as he came to give his second gift; and the Brownie spoke more kindly than before.

"One more trial, Thistle, and she will awake. Go bravely forth and win your last and hardest gift."

Then with a light heart Thistle journeyed away to the brooks and rivers, seeking the Water Spirits. But he looked in vain; till, wandering through the forest where the Brownies took him captive, he stopped beside the quiet lake.

As he stood here he heard a sound of pain, and, looking in the tall grass at his side, he saw the dragon-fly whose kindness he once repaid by pain and sorrow, and who now lay suffering and alone.

Thistle bent tenderly beside him, saying, "Dear Flutter, do not fear me. I will gladly ease your pain, if you will let me; I am your friend, and long to show you how I grieve for all the wrong I did you, when you were so kind to me. Forgive, and let me help and comfort you."

Then he bound up the broken wing, and spoke so tenderly that Flutter doubted him no longer, and was his friend again.

Day by day did Thistle watch beside him, making little beds of cool, fresh moss for him to rest upon, fanning him when he slept, and singing sweet songs to cheer him when awake. And often when poor Flutter longed to be dancing once again over the blue waves, the Fairy bore him in his arms to the lake, and on a broad leaf, with a green flag for a sail, they floated on the still water; while the dragon-fly's companions flew about them, playing merry games.

At length the broken wing was well, and Thistle said he must again seek the Water Spirits. "I can tell you where to find them," said Flutter; "you must follow yonder little brook, and it will lead you to the sea, where the Spirits dwell. I would gladly do more for you, dear Thistle, but I cannot, for they live deep beneath the waves. You will find some kind friend to aid you on your way; and so farewell."

Thistle followed the little brook, as it flowed through field and valley, growing ever larger, till it reached the sea. Here the wind blew freshly, and the great waves rolled and broke at Thistle's feet, as he stood upon the shore, watching the billows dancing and sparkling in the sun.

"How shall I find the Spirits in this great sea, with none to help or guide me? Yet it is my last task, and for Lily-Bell's sake I must not fear or falter now," said Thistle. So he flew hither and thither over the sea, looking through the waves. Soon he saw, far below, the branches of the coral tree.

"They must be here," thought he, and, folding his wings, he plunged into the deep, cold sea. But he saw only fearful monsters and dark shapes that gathered round him; and, trembling with fear, he struggled up again.

The great waves tossed him to and fro, and cast him bruised and faint upon the shore. Here he lay weeping bitterly, till a voice beside him said, "Poor little Elf, what has befallen you? These rough waves are not fit playmates for so delicate a thing as you. Tell me your sorrow, and I will comfort you."

And Thistle, looking up, saw a white sea-bird at his side, who tried with friendly words to cheer him. So he told all his wanderings, and how he sought the Sea Spirits.

"Surely, if bee and blossom do their part to help you, birds should aid you too," said the Sea-bird. "I will call my friend, the Nautilus, and he will bear you safely to the Coral Palace where the Spirits dwell."

So, spreading his great wings, he flew away, and soon Thistle saw a little boat come dancing over the waves, and wait beside the shore for him.

In he sprang. Nautilus raised his little sail to the wind, and the light boat glided swiftly over the blue sea. At last Thistle cried, "I see lovely arches far below; let me go, it is the Spirits' home."

"Nay, close your eyes, and trust to me. I will bear you safely down," said Nautilus.

So Thistle closed his eyes, and listened to the murmur of the sea, as they sank slowly through the waves. The soft sound lulled him to sleep, and when he awoke the boat was gone, and he stood among the Water Spirits, in their strange and lovely home.

Lofty arches of snow-white coral bent above him, and the walls of brightly tinted shells were wreathed with lovely sea-flowers, and the sunlight shining on the waves cast silvery shadows on the ground, where sparkling stones glowed in the sand. A cool, fresh wind swept through the waving garlands of bright sea-moss, and the distant murmur of dashing waves came softly on the air. Soon troops of graceful Spirits flitted by, and when they found the wondering Elf, they gathered round him, bringing pearl-shells heaped with precious stones, and all the rare, strange gifts that lie beneath the sea. But Thistle wished for none of these, and when his tale was told, the kindly Spirits pitied him; and little Pearl sighed, as she told him of the long and weary task he must perform, ere he could win a crown of snow-white pearls like those they wore. But Thistle had gained strength and courage in his wanderings, and did not falter now, when they led him to a place among the coral-workers, and told him he must labor here, till the spreading branches reached the light and air, through the waves that danced above.

With a patient hope that he might yet be worthy of Lily-Bell, the Fairy left the lovely spirits and their pleasant home, to toil among the coral-builders, where all was strange and dim. Long, long, he worked; but still the waves rolled far above them, and his task was not yet done; and many bitter tears poor Thistle shed, and sadly he pined for air and sunlight, the voice of birds, and breath of flowers. Often, folded in the magic garments which the Spirits gave him, that he might pass unharmed among the fearful creatures dwelling there, he rose to the surface of the sea, and, gliding through the waves, gazed longingly upon the hills, now looking blue and dim so far away, or watched the flocks of summer birds, journeying to a warmer land; and they brought sad memories of green old forests, and sunny fields, to the lonely little Fairy floating on the great, wild sea.

Day after day went by, and slowly Thistle's task drew towards an end. Busily toiled the coral-workers, but more busily toiled he; insect and Spirit daily wondered more and more, at the industry and patience of the silent little Elf, who had a friendly word for all, though he never joined them in their sport.

Higher and higher grew the coral-boughs, and lighter grew the Fairy's heart, while thoughts of dear Lily-Bell cheered him on, as day by day he steadily toiled; and when at length the sun shone on his work, and it was done, he stayed but to take the garland he had won, and to thank the good Spirits for their love and care. Then up through the cold, blue waves he swiftly glided, and, shaking the bright drops from his wings, soared singing up to the sunny sky.

On through the fragrant air went Thistle, looking with glad face upon the fair, fresh earth below, where flowers looked smiling up, and green trees bowed their graceful heads as if to welcome him. Soon the forest where Lily-Bell lay sleeping rose before him, and as he passed along the cool, dim wood-paths, never had they seemed so fair.

But when he came where his little friend had slept, it was no longer the dark, silent spot where he last saw her. Garlands hung from every tree, and the fairest flowers filled the air with their sweet breath. Bird's gay voices echoed far and wide, and the little brook went singing by, beneath the arching ferns that bent above it; green leaves rustled in the summer wind, and the air was full of music. But the fairest sight was Lily-Bell, as she lay on the couch of velvet moss that Fairy hands had spread. The golden flower lay beside her, and the glittering robe was folded round her little form. The warmest sunlight fell upon her, and the softest breezes lifted her shining hair.

Happy tears fell fast, as Thistle folded his arms around her, crying, "O Lily-Bell, dear Lily-Bell, awake! I have been true to you, and now my task is done."

Then, with a smile, Lily-Bell awoke, and looked with wondering eyes upon the beauty that had risen round her.

"Dear Thistle, what mean these fair things, and why are we in this lovely place?"

"Listen, Lily-Bell," said the Brownie King, as he appeared beside her. And then he told all that Thistle had done to show his love for her; how he had wandered far and wide to seek the Fairy gifts, and toiled long and hard to win them; how he had been loving, true, and tender, when most lonely and forsaken.

"Bird, bee, and blossom have forgiven him, and none is more loved and trusted now by all, than the once cruel Thistle," said the King, as he bent down to the happy Elf, who bowed low before him.

"You have learned the beauty of a gentle, kindly heart, dear Thistle; and you are now worthy to become the friend of her for whom you have done so much. Place the crown upon her head, for she is Queen of all the Forest Fairies now."

And as the crown shone on the head that Lily-Bell bent down on Thistle's breast, the forest seemed alive with little forms, who sprang from flower and leaf, and gathered round her, bringing gifts for their new Queen.

"If I am Queen, then you are King, dear Thistle," said the Fairy. "Take the crown, and I will have a wreath of flowers. You have toiled and suffered for my sake, and you alone should rule over these little Elves whose love you have won."

"Keep your crown, Lily-Bell, for yonder come the Spirits with their gifts to Thistle," said the Brownie. And, as he pointed with his wand, out from among the mossy roots of an old tree came trooping the Earth Spirits, their flower-bells ringing softly as they came, and their jewelled garments glittering in the sun. On to where Thistledown stood beneath the shadow of the flowers, with Lily-Bell beside him, went the Spirits; and then forth sprang little Sparkle, waving a golden flower, whose silvery music filled the air. "Dear Thistle," said the shining Spirit, "what you toiled so faithfully to win for another, let us offer now as a token of our love for you."

As she ceased, down through the air came floating bands of lovely Air Spirits, bringing a shining robe, and they too told their love for the gentle Fairy who had dwelt with them.

Then softly on the breeze came distant music, growing ever nearer, till over the rippling waves came the singing Water Spirits, in their boats of many-colored shells; and as they placed their glittering crown on Thistle's head, loud rang the flowers, and joyously sang the birds, while all the Forest Fairies cried, with silvery voices, "Lily-Bell and Thistledown! Long live our King and Queen!"

"Have you a tale for us too, dear Violet-Eye?" said the Queen, as Zephyr ceased. The little Elf thus named looked from among the flower-leaves where she sat, and with a smile replied, "As I was weaving garlands in the field, I heard a primrose tell this tale to her friend Golden-Rod."

LITTLE ANNIE'S DREAM;

OR, THE FAIRY FLOWER

*I*n a large and pleasant garden sat little Annie all alone, and she seemed very sad, for drops that were not dew fell fast upon the flowers beside her, who looked wonderingly up, and bent still nearer, as if they longed to cheer and comfort her. The warm wind lifted up her shining hair and softly kissed her cheek, while the sunbeams, looking most kindly in her face, made little rainbows in her tears, and lingered lovingly about her. But Annie paid no heed to sun, or wind, or flower; still the bright tears fell, and she forgot all but her sorrow.

"Little Annie, tell me why you weep," said a low voice in her ear; and, looking up, the child beheld a little figure standing on a vine-leaf at her side; a lovely face smiled on her, from amid bright locks of hair, and shining wings were folded on a white and glittering robe, that fluttered in the wind.

"Who are you, lovely little thing?" cried Annie, smiling through her tears.

"I am a Fairy, little child, and am come to help and comfort you; now tell me why you weep, and let me be your friend," replied the spirit, as she smiled more kindly still on Annie's wondering face.

"And are you really, then, a little Elf, such as I read of in my fairy books? Do you ride on butterflies, sleep in flower-cups, and live among the clouds?"

"Yes, all these things I do, and many stranger still, that all your fairy books can never tell; but now, dear Annie," said the Fairy, bending nearer, "tell me why I found no sunshine on your face; why are these great drops shining on the flowers, and why do you sit alone when BIRD and BEE are calling you to play?"

"Ah, you will not love me any more if I should tell you all," said Annie, while the tears began to fall again; "I am not happy, for I am not good; how shall I learn to be a patient, gentle child? good little Fairy, will you teach me how?"

"Gladly will I aid you, Annie, and if you truly wish to be a happy child, you first must learn to conquer many passions that you cherish now, and make your heart a home for gentle feelings and happy thoughts; the task is hard, but I will give this fairy flower to help and counsel you. Bend hither, that I may place it in your breast; no hand can take it hence, till I unsay the spell that holds it there."

As thus she spoke, the Elf took from her bosom a graceful flower, whose snow-white leaves shone with a strange, soft light. "This is a fairy flower," said the Elf, "invisible to every eye save yours; now listen while I tell its power, Annie. When your heart is filled with loving thoughts, when some kindly deed has been done, some duty well performed, then from the flower there will arise the sweetest, softest fragrance, to reward and gladden you. But when an unkind word is on your lips, when a selfish, angry feeling rises in your heart, or an unkind, cruel deed is to be done, then will you hear the soft, low chime of the flower-bell; listen to its warning, let the word remain unspoken, the deed undone, and in the quiet joy of your own heart, and the magic perfume of your bosom flower, you will find a sweet reward."

"O kind and generous Fairy, how can I ever thank you for this lovely gift!" cried Annie. "I will be true, and listen to my little bell whenever it may ring. But shall I never see YOU more? Ah! if you would only stay with me, I should indeed be good."

"I cannot stay now, little Annie," said the Elf, "but when another Spring comes round, I shall be here again, to see how well the fairy gift has done its work. And now farewell, dear child; be faithful to yourself, and the magic flower will never fade."

Then the gentle Fairy folded her little arms around Annie's neck, laid a soft kiss on her cheek, and, spreading wide her shining wings, flew singing up among the white clouds floating in the sky.

And little Annie sat among her flowers, and watched with wondering joy the fairy blossom shining on her breast.

The pleasant days of Spring and Summer passed away, and in little Annie's garden Autumn flowers were blooming everywhere, with each day's sun and dew growing still more beautiful and bright; but the fairy flower, that should have been the loveliest of all, hung pale and drooping on little Annie's bosom; its fragrance seemed quite gone, and the clear, low music of its warning chime rang often in her ear.

When first the Fairy placed it there, she had been pleased with her new gift, and for a while obeyed the fairy bell, and often tried to win some fragrance from the flower, by kind and pleasant words and actions; then, as the Fairy said, she found a sweet reward in the strange, soft perfume of the magic blossom, as it shone upon her breast; but selfish thoughts would come to tempt her, she would yield, and unkind words fell from her lips; and then the flower drooped pale and scentless, the fairy bell rang mournfully, Annie would forget her better resolutions, and be again a selfish, wilful little child.

At last she tried no longer, but grew angry with the faithful flower, and would have torn it from her breast; but the fairy spell still held it fast, and all her angry words but made it ring a louder, sadder peal. Then she paid no heed to the silvery music sounding in her ear, and each day grew still more unhappy, discontented, and unkind; so, when the Autumn days came round, she was no better for the gentle Fairy's gift, and longed for Spring, that it might be returned; for now the constant echo of the mournful music made her very sad.

One sunny morning, when the fresh, cool Winds were blowing, and not a cloud was in the sky, little Annie walked among her flowers, looking carefully into each, hoping thus to find the Fairy, who alone could take the magic blossom from her breast. But she lifted up their drooping leaves, peeped into their dewy cups in vain; no little Elf lay hidden there, and she turned sadly from them all, saying, "I will go out into the fields and woods, and seek her there. I will not listen to this tiresome music more, nor wear this withered flower longer." So out into the fields she went, where the long grass rustled as she passed, and timid birds looked at her from their nests; where lovely wild-flowers nodded in the wind, and opened wide their fragrant leaves, to welcome in the murmuring bees, while butterflies, like winged flowers, danced and glittered in the sun.

Little Annie looked, searched, and asked them all if any one could tell her of the Fairy whom she sought; but the birds looked wonderingly at her with their soft, bright eyes, and still sang on; the flowers nodded wisely on their stems, but did not speak, while butterfly and bee buzzed and fluttered away, one far too busy, the other too idle, to stay and tell her what she asked.

Then she went through broad fields of yellow grain, that waved around her like a golden forest; here crickets chirped, grasshoppers leaped, and busy ants worked, but they could not tell her what she longed to know.

"Now will I go among the hills," said Annie, "she may be there." So up and down the green hill-sides went her little feet; long she searched and vainly she called; but still no Fairy came. Then by the river-side she went, and asked the gay dragon-flies, and the cool white lilies, if the Fairy had been there; but the blue waves rippled on the white sand at her feet, and no voice answered her.

Then into the forest little Annie went; and as she passed along the dim, cool paths, the wood-flowers smiled up in her face, gay squirrels peeped at her, as they swung amid the vines, and doves cooed softly as she wandered by; but none could answer her. So, weary with her long and useless search, she sat amid the ferns, and feasted on the rosy strawberries that grew beside her, watching meanwhile the crimson evening clouds that glowed around the setting sun.

The night-wind rustled through the boughs, rocking the flowers to sleep; the wild birds sang their evening hymns, and all within the wood grew calm and still; paler and paler grew the purple light, lower and lower drooped little Annie's head, the tall ferns bent to shield her from the dew, the whispering pines sang a soft lullaby; and when the Autumn moon rose up, her silver light shone on the child, where, pillowed on green moss, she lay asleep amid the wood-flowers in the dim old forest.

And all night long beside her stood the Fairy she had sought, and by elfin spell and charm sent to the sleeping child this dream.

Little Annie dreamed she sat in her own garden, as she had often sat before, with angry feelings in her heart, and unkind words upon her lips. The magic flower was ringing its soft warning, but she paid no heed to anything, save her own troubled thoughts; thus she sat, when suddenly a low voice whispered in her ear,—

"Little Annie, look and see the evil things that you are cherishing; I will clothe in fitting shapes the thoughts and feelings that now dwell within your heart, and you shall see how great their power becomes, unless you banish them for ever."

Then Annie saw, with fear and wonder, that the angry words she uttered changed to dark, unlovely forms, each showing plainly from what fault or passion it had sprung. Some of the shapes had scowling faces and bright, fiery eyes; these were the spirits of Anger. Others, with sullen, anxious looks, seemed gathering up all they could reach, and Annie saw that the more they gained, the less they seemed to have; and these she knew were shapes of Selfishness. Spirits of Pride were there, who folded their shadowy garments round them, and turned scornfully away from all the rest. These and many others little Annie saw, which had come from her own heart, and taken form before her eyes.

When first she saw them, they were small and weak; but as she looked they seemed to grow and gather strength, and each gained a strange power over her. She could not drive them from her sight, and they grew ever stronger, darker, and more unlovely to her eyes. They seemed to cast black shadows over all around, to dim the sunshine, blight the flowers, and drive away all bright and lovely things; while rising slowly round her Annie saw a high, dark wall, that seemed to shut out everything she loved; she dared not move, or speak, but, with a strange fear at her heart, sat watching the dim shapes that hovered round her.

Higher and higher rose the shadowy wall, slowly the flowers near her died, lingeringly the sunlight faded; but at last they both were gone, and left her all alone behind the gloomy wall. Then the spirits gathered round her, whispering strange things in her ear, bidding her obey, for by her own will she had yielded up her heart to be their home, and she was now their slave. Then she could hear no more, but, sinking down among the withered flowers, wept sad and bitter tears, for her lost liberty and joy; then through the gloom there shone a faint, soft light, and on her breast she saw her fairy flower, upon whose snow-white leaves her tears lay shining.

Clearer and brighter grew the radiant light, till the evil spirits turned away to the dark shadow of the wall, and left the child alone.

The light and perfume of the flower seemed to bring new strength to Annie, and she rose up, saying, as she bent to kiss the blossom on her breast, "Dear flower, help and guide me now, and I will listen to your voice, and cheerfully obey my faithful fairy bell."

Then in her dream she felt how hard the spirits tried to tempt and trouble her, and how, but for her flower, they would have led her back, and made all dark and dreary as before. Long and hard she struggled, and tears often fell; but after each new trial, brighter shone her magic flower, and sweeter grew its breath, while the spirits lost still more their power to tempt her. Meanwhile, green, flowering vines crept up the high, dark wall, and hid its roughness from her sight; and over these she watched most tenderly, for soon, wherever green leaves and flowers bloomed, the wall beneath grew weak, and fell apart. Thus little Annie worked and hoped, till one by one the evil spirits fled away, and in their place came shining forms, with gentle eyes and smiling lips, who gathered round her with such loving words, and brought such strength and joy to Annie's heart, that nothing evil dared to enter in; while slowly sank the gloomy wall, and, over wreaths of fragrant flowers, she passed out into the pleasant world again, the fairy gift no longer pale and drooping, but now shining like a star upon her breast.

Then the low voice spoke again in Annie's sleeping ear, saying, "The dark, unlovely passions you have looked upon are in your heart; watch well while they are few and weak, lest they should darken your whole life, and shut out love and happiness for ever. Remember well the lesson of the dream, dear child, and let the shining spirits make your heart their home."

And with that voice sounding in her ear, little Annie woke to find it was a dream; but like other dreams it did not pass away; and as she sat alone, bathed in the rosy morning light, and watched the forest waken into life, she thought of the strange forms she had seen, and, looking down upon the flower on her breast, she silently resolved to strive, as she had striven in her dream, to bring back light and beauty to its faded leaves, by being what the Fairy hoped to render her, a patient, gentle little child. And as the thought came to her mind, the flower raised its drooping head, and, looking up into the earnest little face bent over it, seemed by its fragrant breath to answer Annie's silent thought, and strengthen her for what might come.

Meanwhile the forest was astir, birds sang their gay good-morrows from tree to tree, while leaf and flower turned to greet the sun, who rose up smiling on the world; and so beneath the forest boughs and through the dewy fields went little Annie home, better and wiser for her dream.

Autumn flowers were dead and gone, yellow leaves lay rustling on the ground, bleak winds went whistling through the naked trees, and cold, white Winter snow fell softly down; yet now, when all without looked dark and dreary, on little Annie's breast the fairy flower bloomed more beautiful than ever. The memory of her forest dream had never passed away, and through trial and temptation she had been true, and kept her resolution still unbroken; seldom now did the warning bell sound in her ear, and seldom did the flower's fragrance cease to float about her, or the fairy light to brighten all whereon it fell.

So, through the long, cold Winter, little Annie dwelt like a sunbeam in her home, each day growing richer in the love of others, and happier in herself; often was she tempted, but, remembering her dream, she listened only to the music of the fairy bell, and the unkind thought or feeling fled away, the smiling spirits of gentleness and love nestled in her heart, and all was bright again.

So better and happier grew the child, fairer and sweeter grew the flower, till Spring came smiling over the earth, and woke the flowers, set free the streams, and welcomed back the birds; then daily did the happy child sit among her flowers, longing for the gentle Elf to come again, that she might tell her gratitude for all the magic gift had done.

At length, one day, as she sat singing in the sunny nook where all her fairest flowers bloomed, weary with gazing at the far-off sky for the little form she hoped would come, she bent to look with joyful love upon her bosom flower; and as she looked, its folded leaves spread wide apart, and, rising slowly from the deep white cup, appeared the smiling face of the lovely Elf whose coming she had waited for so long.

"Dear Annie, look for me no longer; I am here on your own breast, for you have learned to love my gift, and it has done its work most faithfully and well," the Fairy said, as she looked into the happy child's bright face, and laid her little arms most tenderly about her neck.

"And now have I brought another gift from Fairy-Land, as a fit reward for you, dear child," she said, when Annie had told all her gratitude and love; then, touching the child with her shining wand, the Fairy bid her look and listen silently.

And suddenly the world seemed changed to Annie; for the air was filled with strange, sweet sounds, and all around her floated lovely forms. In every flower sat little smiling Elves, singing gayly as they rocked amid the leaves. On every breeze, bright, airy spirits came floating by; some fanned her cheek with their cool breath, and waved her long hair to and fro, while others rang the flower-bells, and made a pleasant rustling among the leaves. In the fountain, where the water danced and sparkled in the sun, astride of every drop she saw merry little spirits, who plashed and floated in the clear, cool waves, and sang as gayly as the flowers, on whom they scattered glittering dew. The tall trees, as their branches rustled in the wind, sang a low, dreamy song, while the waving grass was filled with little voices she had never heard before. Butterflies whispered lovely tales in her ear, and birds sang cheerful songs in a sweet language she had never understood before. Earth and air seemed filled with beauty and with music she had never dreamed of until now.

"O tell me what it means, dear Fairy! is it another and a lovelier dream, or is the earth in truth so beautiful as this?" she cried, looking with wondering joy upon the Elf, who lay upon the flower in her breast.

"Yes, it is true, dear child," replied the Fairy, "and few are the mortals to whom we give this lovely gift; what to you is now so full of music and of light, to others is but a pleasant summer world; they never know the language of butterfly or bird or flower, and they are blind to all that I have given you the power to see. These fair things are your friends and playmates now, and they will teach you many pleasant lessons, and give you many happy hours; while the garden where you once sat, weeping sad and bitter tears, is now brightened by your own happiness, filled with loving friends by your own kindly thoughts and feelings; and thus rendered a pleasant summer home for the gentle, happy child, whose bosom flower will never fade. And now, dear Annie, I must go; but every Springtime, with the earliest flowers, will I come again to visit you, and bring some fairy gift. Guard well the magic flower, that I may find all fair and bright when next I come."

Then, with a kind farewell, the gentle Fairy floated upward through the sunny air, smiling down upon the child, until she vanished in the soft, white clouds, and little Annie stood alone in her enchanted garden, where all was brightened with the radiant light, and fragrant with the perfume of her fairy flower.

When Moonlight ceased, Summer-Wind laid down her rose-leaf fan, and, leaning back in her acorn cup, told this tale of . . .

Edith Wharton

A gilded cage is still a cage. Edith Wharton was born into one and carried it with her much of her life, though it never fit well. The last child and only girl born to the Jones family who supposedly inspired the phrase "keeping up with the Joneses," Wharton was both privileged with and restricted by extreme wealth and social status. Even before she could read, the only thing Wharton really wanted to do was write. All her family and society wanted her to do was marry well. She tried to do both, initially with equal amounts of failure.

When her mother apparently eviscerated an early attempt at fiction writing, Wharton dutifully turned to poetry. Her family indulged her by privately publishing her first collection of poems when she turned sixteen. Soon after, she secretly started writing fiction again, but upheld her social obligations as a debutante. Within a year, she successfully landed a suitor in Henry Steven. She also anonymously published five poems in the *Atlantic Monthly*. Months after the engagement announcement, Steven's mother objected to the marriage due to "an alleged preponderance of intellectuality on the part of the intended bride," according to accounts in the *Town Topics* newspaper. A couple of years later, Wharton accomplished her socially mandated mission and married Edward Wharton, several years her senior, chronically depressed, and the man who would later embezzle a chunk of her inheritance.

Finally free of the constant pressure of the marriage market and out of her mother's controlling house, in many ways, Wharton began her life in earnest. She read and studied under the guidance of Egerton Winthrop. She traveled at will. She eventually divorced (after the embezzlement). She wrote. She wrote fiction. She wrote fiction in bed after breakfast and tossed her pages on the floor for someone else to collate and type. She often distracted herself with the objects she was trained to desire—pretty and opulent houses and gardens and weeks-long parties among the social elite. Wharton knew she didn't fit in that culture and later wrote about the vapidity of it in novels like *The Age of Innocence*. But she never seemed able to step away from it. Edith Wharton never freed herself completely from the cage, even after she got hold of the key.

Afterward

I

Oh, there is one, of course, but you'll never know it."

The assertion, laughingly flung out six months earlier in a bright June garden, came back to Mary Boyne with a sharp perception of its latent significance as she stood, in the December dusk, waiting for the lamps to be brought into the library.

The words had been spoken by their friend Alida Stair, as they sat at tea on her lawn at Pangbourne, in reference to the very house of which the library in question was the central, the pivotal "feature." Mary Boyne and her husband, in quest of a country place in one of the southern or southwestern counties, had, on their arrival in England, carried their problem straight to Alida Stair, who had successfully solved it in her own case; but it was not until they had rejected, almost capriciously, several practical and judicious suggestions that she threw it out: "Well, there's Lyng, in Dorsetshire. It belongs to Hugo's cousins, and you can get it for a song."

The reasons she gave for its being obtainable on these terms—its remoteness from a station, its lack of electric light, hot-water pipes, and other vulgar necessities—were exactly those pleading in its favor with two romantic Americans perversely in search of the economic drawbacks which were associated, in their tradition, with unusual architectural felicities.

"I should never believe I was living in an old house unless I was thoroughly uncomfortable," Ned Boyne, the more extravagant of the two, had jocosely insisted; "the least hint of 'convenience' would make me think it had been bought out of an exhibition, with the pieces numbered, and set up again." And they had proceeded to enumerate, with humorous precision, their various suspicions and exactions, refusing to believe that the house their cousin recommended was really Tudor till they learned it had no heating system, or that the village church was literally in the grounds till she assured them of the deplorable uncertainty of the water supply.

"It's too uncomfortable to be true!" Edward Boyne had continued to exult as the avowal of each disadvantage was successively wrung from her; but he had cut short his rhapsody to ask, with a sudden relapse to distrust: "And the ghost? You've been concealing from us the fact that there is no ghost!"

Mary, at the moment, had laughed with him, yet almost with

her laugh, being possessed of several sets of independent percep-
tions, had noted a sudden flatness of tone in Alida's answering
hilarity.

"Oh, Dorsetshire's full of ghosts, you know."

"Yes, yes; but that won't do. I don't want to have to drive ten
miles to see somebody else's ghost. I want one of my own on the
premises. Is there a ghost at Lyng?"

His rejoinder had made Alida laugh again, and it was then
that she had flung back tantalizingly: "Oh, there is one, of course,
but you'll never know it."

"Never know it?" Boyne pulled her up. "But what in the world
constitutes a ghost except the fact of its being known for one?"

"I can't say. But that's the story."

"That there's a ghost, but that nobody knows it's a ghost?"

"Well—not till afterward, at any rate."

"Till afterward?"

"Not till long, long afterward."

"But if it's once been identified as an unearthly visitant, why
hasn't its signalement been handed down in the family? How has
it managed to preserve its incognito?"

Alida could only shake her head. "Don't ask me. But it has."

"And then suddenly—" Mary spoke up as if from some cav-
ernous depth of divination—"Suddenly, long afterward, one says
to one's self, 'That was it?'"

She was oddly startled at the sepulchral sound with which
her question fell on the banter of the other two, and she saw the

shadow of the same surprise flit across Alida's clear pupils. "I suppose so. One just has to wait."

"Oh, hang waiting!" Ned broke in. "Life's too short for a ghost who can only be enjoyed in retrospect. Can't we do better than that, Mary?"

But it turned out that in the event they were not destined to, for within three months of their conversation with Mrs. Stair they were established at Lyng, and the life they had yearned for to the point of planning it out in all its daily details had actually begun for them.

It was to sit, in the thick December dusk, by just such a wide-hooded fireplace, under just such black oak rafters, with the sense that beyond the mullioned panes the downs were darkening to a deeper solitude: it was for the ultimate indulgence in such sensations that Mary Boyne had endured for nearly fourteen years the soul-deadening ugliness of the Middle West, and that Boyne had ground on doggedly at his engineering till, with a suddenness that still made her blink, the prodigious windfall of the Blue Star Mine had put them at a stroke in possession of life and the leisure to taste it. They had never for a moment meant their new state to be one of idleness; but they meant to give themselves only to harmonious activities. She had her vision of painting and gardening against a background of gray walls, he dreamed of the production of his long-planned book on the "Economic Basis of Culture"; and with such absorbing work ahead no existence could be too sequestered; they could not get far enough from the world, or plunge deep enough into the past.

Dorsetshire had attracted them from the first by a semblance of remoteness out of all proportion to its geographical position. But to the Boynes it was one of the ever-recurring wonders of the whole incredibly compressed island—a nest of counties, as they put it—that for the production of its effects so little of a given quality went so far: that so few miles made a distance, and so short a distance a difference.

"It's that," Ned had once enthusiastically explained, "that gives such depth to their effects, such relief to their least contrasts. They've been able to lay the butter so thick on every exquisite mouthful."

The butter had certainly been laid on thick at Lyng: the old gray house, hidden under a shoulder of the downs, had almost all the finer marks of commerce with a protracted past. The mere fact that it was neither large nor exceptional made it, to the Boynes, abound the more richly in its special sense—the sense of having been for centuries a deep, dim reservoir of life. The life had probably not been of the most vivid order: for long periods, no doubt, it had fallen as noiselessly into the past as the quiet drizzle of autumn fell, hour after hour, into the green fish-pond between the yews; but these back-waters of existence sometimes breed, in their sluggish depths, strange acuities of emotion, and Mary Boyne had felt from the first the occasional brush of an intenser memory.

The feeling had never been stronger than on the December

afternoon when, waiting in the library for the belated lamps, she rose from her seat and stood among the shadows of the hearth. Her husband had gone off, after luncheon, for one of his long tramps on the downs. She had noticed of late that he preferred to be unaccompanied on these occasions; and, in the tried security of their personal relations, had been driven to conclude that his book was bothering him, and that he needed the afternoons to turn over in solitude the problems left from the morning's work. Certainly the book was not going as smoothly as she had imagined it would, and the lines of perplexity between his eyes had never been there in his engineering days. Then he had often looked fagged to the verge of illness, but the native demon of "worry" had never branded his brow. Yet the few pages he had so far read to her—the introduction, and a synopsis of the opening chapter—gave evidences of a firm possession of his subject, and a deepening confidence in his powers.

The fact threw her into deeper perplexity, since, now that he had done with "business" and its disturbing contingencies, the one other possible element of anxiety was eliminated. Unless it were his health, then? But physically he had gained since they had come to Dorsetshire, grown robuster, ruddier, and fresher-eyed. It was only within a week that she had felt in him the undefinable change that made her restless in his absence, and as tongue-tied in his presence as though it were she who had a secret to keep from him!

The thought that there was a secret somewhere between

them struck her with a sudden smart rap of wonder, and she looked about her down the dim, long room.

"Can it be the house?" she mused.

The room itself might have been full of secrets. They seemed to be piling themselves up, as evening fell, like the layers and layers of velvet shadow dropping from the low ceiling, the dusky walls of books, the smoke-blurred sculpture of the hooded hearth.

"Why, of course—the house is haunted!" she reflected.

The ghost—Alida's imperceptible ghost—after figuring largely in the banter of their first month or two at Lyng, had been gradually discarded as too ineffectual for imaginative use. Mary had, indeed, as became the tenant of a haunted house, made the customary inquiries among her few rural neighbors, but, beyond a vague, "They du say so, Ma'am," the villagers had nothing to impart. The elusive specter had apparently never had sufficient identity for a legend to crystallize about it, and after a time the Boynes had laughingly set the matter down to their profit-and-loss account, agreeing that Lyng was one of the few houses good enough in itself to dispense with supernatural enhancements.

"And I suppose, poor, ineffectual demon, that's why it beats its beautiful wings in vain in the void," Mary had laughingly concluded.

"Or, rather," Ned answered, in the same strain, "why, amid so much that's ghostly, it can never affirm its separate existence as the ghost." And thereupon their invisible housemate had finally dropped out of their references, which were numerous enough to make them promptly unaware of the loss.

Now, as she stood on the hearth, the subject of their earlier curiosity revived in her with a new sense of its meaning—a sense gradually acquired through close daily contact with the scene of the lurking mystery. It was the house itself, of course, that possessed the ghost-seeing faculty, that communed visually but secretly with its own past; and if one could only get into close enough communion with the house, one might surprise its secret, and acquire the ghost-sight on one's own account. Perhaps, in his long solitary hours in this very room, where she never trespassed till the afternoon, her husband had acquired it already, and was silently carrying the dread weight of whatever it had revealed to him. Mary was too well-versed in the code of the spectral world not to know that one could not talk about the ghosts one saw: to do so was almost as great a breach of good breeding as to name a lady in a club. But this explanation did not really satisfy her. "What, after all, except for the fun of the frisson," she reflected, "would he really care for any of their old ghosts?" And thence she was thrown back once more on the fundamental dilemma: the fact that one's greater or less susceptibility to spectral influences had no particular bearing on the case, since, when one did see a ghost at Lyng, one did not know it.

"Not till long afterward," Alida Stair had said. Well, supposing Ned had seen one when they first came, and had known only within the last week what had happened to him? More and more under the spell of the hour, she threw back her searching thoughts to the early days of their tenancy, but at first only to recall a gay confusion of unpacking, settling, arranging of books, and calling to each other from remote corners of the house as treasure after treasure of their habitation revealed itself to them. It was in this particular connection that she presently recalled a certain soft afternoon of the previous October, when, passing from the first rapturous flurry of exploration to a detailed inspection of the old house, she had pressed like a novel heroine a panel that opened at her touch, on a narrow flight of stairs leading to an unsuspected flat ledge of the roof—the roof which, from below, seemed to slope away on all sides too abruptly for any but practised feet to scale.

The view from this hidden coign was enchanting, and she had flown down to snatch Ned from his papers and give him the freedom of her discovery. She remembered still how, standing on the narrow ledge, he had passed his arm about her while their gaze flew to the long, tossed horizon-line of the downs, and then dropped contentedly back to trace the arabesque of yew hedges about the fish-pond, and the shadow of the cedar on the lawn.

"And now the other way," he had said, gently turning her about within his arm; and closely pressed to him, she had absorbed, like some long, satisfying draft, the picture of the gray-walled court, the squat lions on the gates, and the lime-avenue reaching up to the highroad under the downs.

It was just then, while they gazed and held each other, that she had felt his arm relax, and heard a sharp "Hullo!" that made her turn to glance at him.

Distinctly, yes, she now recalled she had seen, as she glanced, a shadow of anxiety, of perplexity, rather, fall across his face; and, following his eyes, had beheld the figure of a man—a man in loose, grayish clothes, as it appeared to her—who was sauntering down the lime-avenue to the court with the tentative gait of a stranger seeking his way. Her short-sighted eyes had given her but a blurred impression of slightness and grayness, with something foreign, or at least unlocal, in the cut of the figure or its garb; but her husband had apparently seen more—seen enough to make him push past her with a sharp "Wait!" and dash down the twisting stairs without pausing to give her a hand for the descent.

A slight tendency to dizziness obliged her, after a provisional clutch at the chimney against which they had been leaning, to follow him down more cautiously; and when she had reached the attic landing she paused again for a less definite reason, leaning over the oak banister to strain her eyes through the silence of the brown, sun-flecked depths below. She lingered there till, somewhere in those depths, she heard the closing of a door; then, mechanically impelled, she went down the shallow flights of steps till she reached the lower hall.

The front door stood open on the mild sunlight of the court, and hall and court were empty. The library door was open, too, and after listening in vain for any sound of voices within, she quickly crossed the threshold, and found her husband alone, vaguely fingering the papers on his desk.

He looked up, as if surprised at her precipitate entrance, but the shadow of anxiety had passed from his face, leaving it even, as she fancied, a little brighter and clearer than usual.

"What was it? Who was it?" she asked.

"Who?" he repeated, with the surprise still all on his side.

"The man we saw coming toward the house."

He seemed honestly to reflect. "The man? Why, I thought I saw Peters; I dashed after him to say a word about the stable-drains, but he had disappeared before I could get down."

"Disappeared? Why, he seemed to be walking so slowly when we saw him."

Boyne shrugged his shoulders. "So I thought; but he must have got up steam in the interval. What do you say to our trying a scramble up Meldon Steep before sunset?"

That was all. At the time the occurrence had been less than nothing, had, indeed, been immediately obliterated by the magic of their first vision from Meldon Steep, a height which they had dreamed of climbing ever since they had first seen its bare spine heaving itself above the low roof of Lyng. Doubtless it was the mere fact of the other incident's having occurred on the very day of their ascent to Meldon that had kept it stored away in the unconscious fold of association from which it now emerged; for in itself it had no mark of the portentous. At the moment there could have been nothing more natural than that Ned should dash himself from the roof in the pursuit of dilatory tradesmen. It was the period when they were always on the watch for one or the other of the specialists employed about the place; always lying in wait for them, and dashing out at them with questions, reproaches, or reminders. And certainly in the distance the gray figure had looked like Peters.

Yet now, as she reviewed the rapid scene, she felt her husband's explanation of it to have been invalidated by the look of anxiety on his face. Why had the familiar appearance of Peters made him anxious? Why, above all, if it was of such prime necessity to confer with that authority on the subject of the stable-drains, had the failure to find him produced such a look of relief? Mary could not say that any one of these considerations had occurred to her at the time, yet, from the promptness with which they now marshaled themselves at her summons, she had a sudden sense that they must all along have been there, waiting their hour.

II

Weary with her thoughts, she moved toward the window. The library was now completely dark, and she was surprised to see how much faint light the outer world still held.

As she peered out into it across the court, a figure shaped itself in the tapering perspective of bare lines: it looked a mere blot of deeper gray in the grayness, and for an instant, as it moved toward her, her heart thumped to the thought, "It's the ghost!"

She had time, in that long instant, to feel suddenly that the man of whom, two months earlier, she had a brief distant vision from the roof was now, at his predestined hour, about to reveal himself as not having been Peters; and her spirit sank under the impending fear of the disclosure. But almost with the next tick of the clock the ambiguous figure, gaining substance and character, showed itself even to her weak sight as her husband's; and she turned away to meet him, as he entered, with the confession of her folly.

"It's really too absurd," she laughed out from the threshold, "but I never can remember!"

"Remember what?" Boyne questioned as they drew together.

"That when one sees the Lyng ghost one never knows it."

Her hand was on his sleeve, and he kept it there, but with no response in his gesture or in the lines of his fagged, preoccupied face.

"Did you think you'd seen it?" he asked, after an appreciable interval.

"Why, I actually took you for it, my dear, in my mad determination to spot it!"

"Me—just now?" His arm dropped away, and he turned from her with a faint echo of her laugh. "Really, dearest, you'd better give it up, if that's the best you can do."

"Yes, I give it up—I give it up. Have you?" she asked, turning round on him abruptly.

The parlor-maid had entered with letters and a lamp, and the light struck up into Boyne's face as he bent above the tray she presented.

"Have you?" Mary perversely insisted, when the servant had disappeared on her errand of illumination.

"Have I what?" he rejoined absently, the light bringing out the sharp stamp of worry between his brows as he turned over the letters.

"Given up trying to see the ghost." Her heart beat a little at the experiment she was making.

Her husband, laying his letters aside, moved away into the shadow of the hearth.

"I never tried," he said, tearing open the wrapper of a newspaper.

"Well, of course," Mary persisted, "the exasperating thing is that there's no use trying, since one can't be sure till so long afterward."

He was unfolding the paper as if he had hardly heard her; but after a pause, during which the sheets rustled spasmodically between his hands, he lifted his head to say abruptly, "Have you any idea how long?"

Mary had sunk into a low chair beside the fireplace. From her seat she looked up, startled, at her husband's profile, which was darkly projected against the circle of lamplight.

"No; none. Have YOU?" she retorted, repeating her former phrase with an added keenness of intention.

Boyne crumpled the paper into a bunch, and then inconsequently turned back with it toward the lamp.

"Lord, no! I only meant," he explained, with a faint tinge of impatience, "is there any legend, any tradition, as to that?"

"Not that I know of," she answered; but the impulse to add, "What makes you ask?" was checked by the reappearance of the parlor maid with tea and a second lamp.

With the dispersal of shadows, and the repetition of the daily domestic office, Mary Boyne felt herself less oppressed by that sense of something mutely imminent which had darkened her solitary afternoon. For a few moments she gave herself silently to the details of her task, and when she looked up from it she was struck to the point of bewilderment by the change in her husband's face. He had seated himself near the farther lamp, and was absorbed in the perusal of his letters; but was it something he had found in them, or merely the shifting of her own point of view, that had restored his features to their normal aspect? The longer she looked, the more definitely the change affirmed itself. The lines of painful tension had vanished, and such traces of fatigue as lingered were of the kind easily attributable to steady mental effort. He glanced up, as if drawn by her gaze, and met her eyes with a smile.

"I'm dying for my tea, you know; and here's a letter for you," he said.

She took the letter he held out in exchange for the cup she

proffered him, and, returning to her seat, broke the seal with the languid gesture of the reader whose interests are all inclosed in the circle of one cherished presence.

Her next conscious motion was that of starting to her feet, the letter falling to them as she rose, while she held out to her husband a long newspaper clipping.

"Ned! What's this? What does it mean?"

He had risen at the same instant, almost as if hearing her cry before she uttered it; and for a perceptible space of time he and she studied each other, like adversaries watching for an advantage, across the space between her chair and his desk.

"What's what? You fairly made me jump!" Boyne said at length, moving toward her with a sudden, half-exasperated laugh. The shadow of apprehension was on his face again, not now a look of fixed foreboding, but a shifting vigilance of lips and eyes that gave her the sense of his feeling himself invisibly surrounded.

Her hand shook so that she could hardly give him the clipping.

"This article—from the 'Waukesha Sentinel'—that a man named Elwell has brought suit against you—that there was something wrong about the Blue Star Mine. I can't understand more than half."

They continued to face each other as she spoke, and to her astonishment, she saw that her words had the almost immediate effect of dissipating the strained watchfulness of his look.

"Oh, that!" He glanced down the printed slip, and then folded it with the gesture of one who handles something harmless and familiar. "What's the matter with you this afternoon, Mary? I thought you'd got bad news."

She stood before him with her undefinable terror subsiding slowly under the reassuring touch of his composure.

"You knew about this, then—it's all right?"

"Certainly I knew about it; and it's all right."

"But what is it? I don't understand. What does this man accuse you of?"

"Oh, pretty nearly every crime in the calendar." Boyne had tossed the clipping down, and thrown himself comfortably into an arm-chair near the fire. "Do you want to hear the story? It's not particularly interesting—just a squabble over interests in the Blue Star."

"But who is this Elwell? I don't know the name."

"Oh, he's a fellow I put into it—gave him a hand up. I told you all about him at the time."

"I daresay. I must have forgotten." Vainly she strained back among her memories. "But if you helped him, why does he make this return?"

"Oh, probably some shyster lawyer got hold of him and talked him over. It's all rather technical and complicated. I thought that kind of thing bored you."

His wife felt a sting of compunction. Theoretically, she deprecated the American wife's detachment from her husband's professional interests, but in practice she had always found it difficult to fix her attention on Boyne's report of the transactions in

which his varied interests involved him. Besides, she had felt from
the first that, in a community where the amenities of living could
be obtained only at the cost of efforts as arduous as her husband's
professional labors, such brief leisure as they could command
should be used as an escape from immediate preoccupations, a
flight to the life they always dreamed of living. Once or twice,
now that this new life had actually drawn its magic circle about
them, she had asked herself if she had done right; but hitherto
such conjectures had been no more than the retrospective excur-
sions of an active fancy. Now, for the first time, it startled her a
little to find how little she knew of the material foundation on
which her happiness was built.

She glanced again at her husband, and was reassured by
the composure of his face; yet she felt the need of more definite
grounds for her reassurance.

"But doesn't this suit worry you? Why have you never spoken
to me about it?"

He answered both questions at once: "I didn't speak of it at
first because it did worry me—annoyed me, rather. But it's all
ancient history now. Your correspondent must have got hold of a
back number of the 'Sentinel.'"

She felt a quick thrill of relief. "You mean it's over? He's lost
his case?"

There was a just perceptible delay in Boyne's reply. "The
suit's been withdrawn—that's all."

But she persisted, as if to exonerate herself from the inward charge of being too easily put off. "Withdrawn because he saw he had no chance?"

"Oh, he had no chance," Boyne answered.

She was still struggling with a dimly felt perplexity at the back of her thoughts.

"How long ago was it withdrawn?"

He paused, as if with a slight return of his former uncertainty. "I've just had the news now; but I've been expecting it."

"Just now—in one of your letters?"

"Yes; in one of my letters."

She made no answer, and was aware only, after a short interval of waiting, that he had risen, and strolling across the room, had placed himself on the sofa at her side. She felt him, as he did so, pass an arm about her, she felt his hand seek hers and clasp it, and turning slowly, drawn by the warmth of his cheek, she met the smiling clearness of his eyes.

"It's all right—it's all right?" she questioned, through the flood of her dissolving doubts; and "I give you my word it never was righter!" he laughed back at her, holding her close.

III

One of the strangest things she was afterward to recall out of all the next day's incredible strangeness was the sudden and complete recovery of her sense of security.

It was in the air when she woke in her low-ceilinged, dusky room; it accompanied her down-stairs to the breakfast-table, flashed out at her from the fire, and re-duplicated itself brightly from the flanks of the urn and the sturdy flutings of the Georgian teapot. It was as if, in some roundabout way, all her diffused apprehensions of the previous day, with their moment of sharp concentration about the newspaper article,—as if this dim questioning of the future, and startled return upon the past,— had between them liquidated the arrears of some haunting moral obligation. If she had indeed been careless of her husband's affairs, it was, her new state seemed to prove, because her faith in him instinctively justified such carelessness; and his right to her faith had overwhelmingly affirmed itself in the very face of menace and suspicion. She had never seen him more untroubled, more naturally and unconsciously in possession of himself, than after the cross-examination to which she had subjected him: it was almost as if he had been aware of her lurking doubts, and had wanted the air cleared as much as she did.

It was as clear, thank Heaven! as the bright outer light that surprised her almost with a touch of summer when she issued from the house for her daily round of the gardens. She had left Boyne at his desk, indulging herself, as she passed the library door, by a last peep at his quiet face, where he bent, pipe in his mouth, above his papers, and now she had her own morning's task to perform. The task involved on such charmed winter days almost as much delighted loitering about the different quarters of her demesne as if spring were already at work on shrubs and borders. There were such inexhaustible possibilities still before her, such opportunities to bring out the latent graces of the old place, without a single irreverent touch of alteration, that the winter months were all too short to plan what spring and autumn executed. And her recovered sense of safety gave, on this particular morning, a peculiar zest to her progress through the sweet, still place. She went first to the kitchen-garden, where the espaliered pear-trees drew complicated patterns on the walls, and pigeons were fluttering and preening about the silvery-slated roof of their cot. There was something wrong about the piping of the hothouse, and she was expecting an authority from Dorchester, who was to drive out between trains and make a diagnosis of the boiler. But when she dipped into the damp heat of the green-houses, among the spiced scents and waxy pinks and reds of old-fashioned exotics,—even the flora of Lyng was in the note!— she learned that the great man had not arrived, and the day being too rare to waste in an artificial atmosphere, she came out again and paced slowly along the springy turf of the bowling-green to the gardens behind the house. At their farther end rose a grass terrace, commanding, over the fish-pond and the yew hedges, a view of the long house-front, with its twisted chimney-stacks and the blue shadows of its roof angles, all drenched in the pale gold moisture of the air.

Seen thus, across the level tracery of the yews, under the suffused, mild light, it sent her, from its open windows and hospitably smoking chimneys, the look of some warm human presence, of a mind slowly ripened on a sunny wall of experience. She had never before had so deep a sense of her intimacy with it, such a conviction that its secrets were all beneficent, kept, as they said to children, "for one's good," so complete a trust in its power to gather up her life and Ned's into the harmonious pattern of the long, long story it sat there weaving in the sun.

She heard steps behind her, and turned, expecting to see the gardener, accompanied by the engineer from Dorchester. But only one figure was in sight, that of a youngish, slightly built man, who, for reasons she could not on the spot have specified, did not remotely resemble her preconceived notion of an authority on hot-house boilers. The new-comer, on seeing her, lifted his hat, and paused with the air of a gentleman—perhaps a traveler—desirous of having it immediately known that his intrusion is involuntary. The local fame of Lyng occasionally attracted the more intelligent sight-seer, and Mary half-expected to see the stranger dissemble a camera, or justify his presence by producing it. But he made no gesture of any sort, and after a moment she asked, in a tone responding to the courteous deprecation of his attitude: "Is there any one you wish to see?"

"I came to see Mr. Boyne," he replied. His intonation, rather than his accent, was faintly American, and Mary, at the familiar note, looked at him more closely. The brim of his soft felt hat cast a shade on his face, which, thus obscured, wore to her short-sighted gaze a look of seriousness, as of a person arriving "on business," and civilly but firmly aware of his rights.

Past experience had made Mary equally sensible to such claims; but she was jealous of her husband's morning hours, and doubtful of his having given any one the right to intrude on them.

"Have you an appointment with Mr. Boyne?" she asked.

He hesitated, as if unprepared for the question.

"Not exactly an appointment," he replied.

"Then I'm afraid, this being his working-time, that he can't receive you now. Will you give me a message, or come back later?"

The visitor, again lifting his hat, briefly replied that he would come back later, and walked away, as if to regain the front of the house. As his figure receded down the walk between the yew hedges, Mary saw him pause and look up an instant at the peaceful house-front bathed in faint winter sunshine; and it struck her, with a tardy touch of compunction, that it would have been more humane to ask if he had come from a distance, and to offer, in that case, to inquire if her husband could receive him. But as the thought occurred to her he passed out of sight behind a pyramidal yew, and at the same moment her attention was distracted by the approach of the gardener, attended by the bearded pepper-and-salt figure of the boiler-maker from Dorchester.

The encounter with this authority led to such far-reaching issues that they resulted in his finding it expedient to ignore his train, and beguiled Mary into spending the remainder of the morning in absorbed confabulation among the greenhouses. She was startled to find, when the colloquy ended, that it was nearly luncheon-time, and she half expected, as she hurried back to the house, to see her husband coming out to meet her. But she found no one in the court but an under-gardener raking the gravel, and the hall, when she entered it, was so silent that she guessed Boyne to be still at work behind the closed door of the library.

Not wishing to disturb him, she turned into the drawing-room, and there, at her writing-table, lost herself in renewed calculations of the outlay to which the morning's conference had committed her. The knowledge that she could permit herself such follies had not yet lost its novelty; and somehow, in contrast to the vague apprehensions of the previous days, it now seemed an element of her recovered security, of the sense that, as Ned had said, things in general had never been "righter."

She was still luxuriating in a lavish play of figures when the parlor-maid, from the threshold, roused her with a dubiously worded inquiry as to the expediency of serving luncheon. It was one of their jokes that Trimmle announced luncheon as if she were divulging a state secret, and Mary, intent upon her papers, merely murmured an absent-minded assent.

She felt Trimmle wavering expressively on the threshold as if in rebuke of such offhand acquiescence; then her retreating steps sounded down the passage, and Mary, pushing away her papers, crossed the hall, and went to the library door. It was still closed, and she wavered in her turn, disliking to disturb her husband, yet anxious that he should not exceed his normal measure of work.

As she stood there, balancing her impulses, the esoteric Trimmle returned with the announcement of luncheon, and Mary, thus impelled, opened the door and went into the library.

Boyne was not at his desk, and she peered about her, expecting to discover him at the book-shelves, somewhere down the length of the room; but her call brought no response, and gradually it became clear to her that he was not in the library.

She turned back to the parlor-maid.

"Mr. Boyne must be up-stairs. Please tell him that luncheon is ready."

The parlor-maid appeared to hesitate between the obvious duty of obeying orders and an equally obvious conviction of the foolishness of the injunction laid upon her. The struggle resulted in her saying doubtfully, "If you please, Madam, Mr. Boyne's not up-stairs."

"Not in his room? Are you sure?"

"I'm sure, Madam."

Mary consulted the clock. "Where is he, then?"

"He's gone out," Trimmle announced, with the superior air of one who has respectfully waited for the question that a well-ordered mind would have first propounded.

Mary's previous conjecture had been right, then. Boyne must have gone to the gardens to meet her, and since she had missed him, it was clear that he had taken the shorter way by the south door, instead of going round to the court. She crossed the hall to the glass portal opening directly on the yew garden, but the parlor maid, after another moment of inner conflict, decided to bring out recklessly, "Please, Madam, Mr. Boyne didn't go that way."

Mary turned back. "Where did he go? And when?"

"He went out of the front door, up the drive, Madam." It was a matter of principle with Trimmle never to answer more than one question at a time.

"Up the drive? At this hour?" Mary went to the door herself, and glanced across the court through the long tunnel of bare limes. But its perspective was as empty as when she had scanned it on entering the house.

"Did Mr. Boyne leave no message?" she asked.

Trimmle seemed to surrender herself to a last struggle with the forces of chaos.

"No, Madam. He just went out with the gentleman."

"The gentleman? What gentleman?" Mary wheeled about, as if to front this new factor.

"The gentleman who called, Madam," said Trimmle, resignedly.

"When did a gentleman call? Do explain yourself, Trimmle!"

Only the fact that Mary was very hungry, and that she wanted to consult her husband about the greenhouses, would have caused her to lay so unusual an injunction on her attendant; and even now she was detached enough to note in Trimmle's eye the dawning defiance of the respectful subordinate who has been pressed too hard.

"I couldn't exactly say the hour, Madam, because I didn't let the gentleman in," she replied, with the air of magnanimously ignoring the irregularity of her mistress's course.

"You didn't let him in?"

"No, Madam. When the bell rang I was dressing, and Agnes—"

"Go and ask Agnes, then," Mary interjected. Trimmle still wore her look of patient magnanimity. "Agnes would not know, Madam, for she had unfortunately burnt her hand in trying the wick of the new lamp from town—" Trimmle, as Mary was aware, had always been opposed to the new lamp—" and so Mrs. Dockett sent the kitchen-maid instead."

Mary looked again at the clock. "It's after two! Go and ask the kitchen-maid if Mr. Boyne left any word."

She went into luncheon without waiting, and Trimmle presently brought her there the kitchen-maid's statement that the gentleman had called about one o'clock, that Mr. Boyne had gone out with him without leaving any message. The kitchen-maid did not even know the caller's name, for he had written it on a slip of paper, which he had folded and handed to her, with the injunction to deliver it at once to Mr. Boyne.

Mary finished her luncheon, still wondering, and when it was over, and Trimmle had brought the coffee to the drawing-room, her wonder had deepened to a first faint tinge of disquietude. It was unlike Boyne to absent himself without explanation at so unwonted an hour, and the difficulty of identifying the visitor whose summons he had apparently obeyed made his disappearance the more unaccountable. Mary Boyne's experience as the wife of a busy engineer, subject to sudden calls and compelled to keep irregular hours, had trained her to the philosophic acceptance of surprises; but since Boyne's withdrawal from business he had adopted a Benedictine regularity of life. As if to make up for the dispersed and agitated years, with their "stand-up" lunches and dinners rattled down to the joltings of the dining-car, he cultivated the last refinements of punctuality and monotony, discouraging his wife's fancy for the unexpected; and declaring that to a delicate taste there were infinite gradations of pleasure in the fixed recurrences of habit.

Still, since no life can completely defend itself from the unforeseen, it was evident that all Boyne's precautions would sooner or later prove unavailable, and Mary concluded that he had cut short a tiresome visit by walking with his caller to the station, or at least accompanying him for part of the way.

This conclusion relieved her from farther preoccupation, and she went out herself to take up her conference with the gardener. Thence she walked to the village post-office, a mile or so away; and when she turned toward home, the early twilight was setting in.

She had taken a foot-path across the downs, and as Boyne, meanwhile, had probably returned from the station by the highroad, there was little likelihood of their meeting on the way. She felt sure, however, of his having reached the house before her;

so sure that, when she entered it herself, without even pausing to inquire of Trimmle, she made directly for the library. But the library was still empty, and with an unwonted precision of visual memory she immediately observed that the papers on her husband's desk lay precisely as they had lain when she had gone in to call him to luncheon.

Then of a sudden she was seized by a vague dread of the unknown. She had closed the door behind her on entering, and as she stood alone in the long, silent, shadowy room, her dread seemed to take shape and sound, to be there audibly breathing and lurking among the shadows. Her short-sighted eyes strained through them, half discerning an actual presence, something aloof, that watched and knew; and in the recoil from that intangible propinquity she threw herself suddenly on the bell-rope and gave it a desperate pull.

The long, quavering summons brought Trimmle in precipitately with a lamp, and Mary breathed again at this sobering reappearance of the usual.

"You may bring tea if Mr. Boyne is in," she said, to justify her ring.

"Very well, Madam. But Mr. Boyne is not in," said Trimmle, putting down the lamp.

"Not in? You mean he's come back and gone out again?"

"No, Madam. He's never been back."

The dread stirred again, and Mary knew that now it had her fast.

"Not since he went out with—the gentleman?"

"Not since he went out with the gentleman."

"But who was the gentleman?" Mary gasped out, with the sharp note of some one trying to be heard through a confusion of meaningless noises.

"That I couldn't say, Madam." Trimmle, standing there by the lamp, seemed suddenly to grow less round and rosy, as though eclipsed by the same creeping shade of apprehension.

"But the kitchen-maid knows—wasn't it the kitchen-maid who let him in?"

"She doesn't know either, Madam, for he wrote his name on a folded paper."

Mary, through her agitation, was aware that they were both designating the unknown visitor by a vague pronoun, instead of the conventional formula which, till then, had kept their allusions within the bounds of custom. And at the same moment her mind caught at the suggestion of the folded paper.

"But he must have a name! Where is the paper?"

She moved to the desk, and began to turn over the scattered documents that littered it. The first that caught her eye was an unfinished letter in her husband's hand, with his pen lying across it, as though dropped there at a sudden summons.

"My dear Parvis,"—who was Parvis?—"I have just received your letter announcing Elwell's death, and while I suppose there is now no farther risk of trouble, it might be safer—"

She tossed the sheet aside, and continued her search; but

no folded paper was discoverable among the letters and pages of manuscript which had been swept together in a promiscuous heap, as if by a hurried or a startled gesture.

"But the kitchen-maid saw him. Send her here," she commanded, wondering at her dullness in not thinking sooner of so simple a solution.

Trimmle, at the behest, vanished in a flash, as if thankful to be out of the room, and when she reappeared, conducting the agitated underling, Mary had regained her self-possession, and had her questions pat.

The gentleman was a stranger, yes—that she understood. But what had he said? And, above all, what had he looked like? The first question was easily enough answered, for the disconcerting reason that he had said so little—had merely asked for Mr. Boyne, and, scribbling something on a bit of paper, had requested that it should at once be carried in to him.

"Then you don't know what he wrote? You're not sure it was his name?"

The kitchen-maid was not sure, but supposed it was, since he had written it in answer to her inquiry as to whom she should announce.

"And when you carried the paper in to Mr. Boyne, what did he say?"

The kitchen-maid did not think that Mr. Boyne had said anything, but she could not be sure, for just as she had handed him the paper and he was opening it, she had become aware that the visitor had followed her into the library, and she had slipped out, leaving the two gentlemen together.

"But then, if you left them in the library, how do you know that they went out of the house?"

This question plunged the witness into momentary in-articulateness, from which she was rescued by Trimmle, who, by means of ingenious circumlocutions, elicited the statement that before she could cross the hall to the back passage she had heard the gentlemen behind her, and had seen them go out of the front door together.

"Then, if you saw the gentleman twice, you must be able to tell me what he looked like."

But with this final challenge to her powers of expression it became clear that the limit of the kitchen-maid's endurance had been reached. The obligation of going to the front door to "show in" a visitor was in itself so subversive of the fundamental order of things that it had thrown her faculties into hopeless disarray, and she could only stammer out, after various panting efforts at evocation, "His hat, mum, was different-like, as you might say—"

"Different? How different?" Mary flashed out at her, her own mind, in the same instant, leaping back to an image left on it that morning, but temporarily lost under layers of subsequent impressions.

"His hat had a wide brim, you mean? and his face was pale—a youngish face?" Mary pressed her, with a white-lipped intensity of interrogation. But if the kitchen-maid found any adequate answer to this challenge, it was swept away for her listener down the rushing current of her own convictions. The stranger—the stranger in the garden! Why had Mary not thought of him before? She needed no one now to tell her that it was he who had called for her husband and gone away with him. But who was he, and why had Boyne obeyed his call?

IV

It leaped out at her suddenly, like a grin out of the dark, that they had often called England so little—"Such a confoundedly hard place to get lost in."

A confoundedly hard place to get lost in! That had been her husband's phrase. And now, with the whole machinery of official investigation sweeping its flash-lights from shore to shore, and across the dividing straits; now, with Boyne's name blazing from the walls of every town and village, his portrait how that wrung her! hawked up and down the country like the image of a hunted criminal; now the little compact, populous island, so policed, surveyed, and administered, revealed itself as a Sphinx-like guardian of abysmal mysteries, staring back into his wife's anguished eyes as if with the malicious joy of knowing something they would never know!

In the fortnight since Boyne's disappearance there had been

no word of him, no trace of his movements. Even the usual mis-
leading reports that raise expectancy in tortured bosoms had
been few and fleeting. No one but the bewildered kitchen-maid
had seen him leave the house, and no one else had seen "the
gentleman" who accompanied him. All inquiries in the neighbor-
hood failed to elicit the memory of a stranger's presence that
day in the neighborhood of Lyng. And no one had met Edward
Boyne, either alone or in company, in any of the neighboring
villages, or on the road across the downs, or at either of the local
railway-stations. The sunny English noon had swallowed him as
completely as if he had gone out into Cimmerian night.

Mary, while every external means of investigation was work-
ing at its highest pressure, had ransacked her husband's papers
for any trace of antecedent complications, of entanglements or
obligations unknown to her, that might throw a faint ray into
the darkness. But if any such had existed in the background of
Boyne's life, they had disappeared as completely as the slip of
paper on which the visitor had written his name. There remained
no possible thread of guidance except—if it were indeed an
exception—the letter which Boyne had apparently been in the
act of writing when he received his mysterious summons. That
letter, read and reread by his wife, and submitted by her to the
police, yielded little enough for conjecture to feed on.

"I have just heard of Elwell's death, and while I suppose there
is now no farther risk of trouble, it might be safer—" That was
all. The "risk of trouble" was easily explained by the newspaper

clipping which had apprised Mary of the suit brought against her husband by one of his associates in the Blue Star enterprise. The only new information conveyed in the letter was the fact of its showing Boyne, when he wrote it, to be still apprehensive of the results of the suit, though he had assured his wife that it had been withdrawn, and though the letter itself declared that the plaintiff was dead. It took several weeks of exhaustive cabling to fix the identity of the "Parvis" to whom the fragmentary communication was addressed, but even after these inquiries had shown him to be a Waukesha lawyer, no new facts concerning the Elwell suit were elicited. He appeared to have had no direct concern in it, but to have been conversant with the facts merely as an acquaintance, and possible intermediary; and he declared himself unable to divine with what object Boyne intended to seek his assistance.

This negative information, sole fruit of the first fortnight's feverish search, was not increased by a jot during the slow weeks that followed. Mary knew that the investigations were still being carried on, but she had a vague sense of their gradually slackening, as the actual march of time seemed to slacken. It was as though the days, flying horror-struck from the shrouded image of the one inscrutable day, gained assurance as the distance lengthened, till at last they fell back into their normal gait. And so with the human imaginations at work on the dark event. No doubt it occupied them still, but week by week and hour by hour it grew less absorbing, took up less space, was slowly but inevitably crowded out of the foreground of consciousness by the new problems perpetually bubbling up from the vaporous caldron of human experience.

Even Mary Boyne's consciousness gradually felt the same lowering of velocity. It still swayed with the incessant oscillations of conjecture; but they were slower, more rhythmical in their beat. There were moments of overwhelming lassitude when, like the victim of some poison which leaves the brain clear, but holds the body motionless, she saw herself domesticated with the Horror, accepting its perpetual presence as one of the fixed conditions of life.

These moments lengthened into hours and days, till she passed into a phase of stolid acquiescence. She watched the familiar routine of life with the incurious eye of a savage on whom the meaningless processes of civilization make but the faintest impression. She had come to regard herself as part of the routine, a spoke of the wheel, revolving with its motion; she felt almost like the furniture of the room in which she sat, an insensate object to be dusted and pushed about with the chairs and tables. And this deepening apathy held her fast at Lyng, in spite of the urgent entreaties of friends and the usual medical recommendation of "change." Her friends supposed that her refusal to move was inspired by the belief that her husband would one day return to the spot from which he had vanished, and a beautiful legend grew up about this imaginary state of waiting. But in reality she had no such belief: the depths of anguish inclosing her were no longer lighted by flashes of hope. She was sure that Boyne would never come back, that he had gone out of her sight as completely as if Death itself had waited that day on the threshold. She had even renounced, one by one, the various theories as to his disappearance which had been advanced by the press, the police, and her own agonized imagination. In sheer lassitude her mind turned from these alternatives of horror, and sank back into the blank fact that he was gone.

No, she would never know what had become of him—no one would ever know. But the house knew; the library in which she spent her long, lonely evenings knew. For it was here that the last scene had been enacted, here that the stranger had come, and spoken the word which had caused Boyne to rise and follow him. The floor she trod had felt his tread; the books on the shelves had seen his face; and there were moments when the intense consciousness of the old, dusky walls seemed about to break out into some audible revelation of their secret. But the revelation never came, and she knew it would never come. Lyng was not one of the garrulous old houses that betray the secrets intrusted to them. Its very legend proved that it had always been the mute accomplice, the incorruptible custodian of the mysteries it had surprised. And Mary Boyne, sitting face to face with its portentous silence, felt the futility of seeking to break it by any human means.

V

"I don't say it wasn't straight, yet don't say it was straight. It was business."

Mary, at the words, lifted her head with a start, and looked intently at the speaker.

When, half an hour before, a card with "Mr. Parvis" on it had been brought up to her, she had been immediately aware that the name had been a part of her consciousness ever since she had read it at the head of Boyne's unfinished letter. In the library she had found awaiting her a small neutral-tinted man with a bald head and gold eye-glasses, and it sent a strange tremor through her to know that this was the person to whom her husband's last known thought had been directed.

Parvis, civilly, but without vain preamble,—in the manner of a man who has his watch in his hand,—had set forth the object of his visit. He had "run over" to England on business, and finding himself in the neighborhood of Dorchester, had not wished to leave it without paying his respects to Mrs. Boyne; without asking her, if the occasion offered, what she meant to do about Bob Elwell's family.

The words touched the spring of some obscure dread in Mary's bosom. Did her visitor, after all, know what Boyne had meant by his unfinished phrase? She asked for an elucidation of his question, and noticed at once that he seemed surprised at her continued ignorance of the subject. Was it possible that she really knew as little as she said?

"I know nothing—you must tell me," she faltered out; and her visitor thereupon proceeded to unfold his story. It threw, even to her confused perceptions, and imperfectly initiated vision, a lurid glare on the whole hazy episode of the Blue Star Mine. Her husband had made his money in that brilliant speculation at the cost of "getting ahead" of some one less alert to seize the chance; the victim of his ingenuity was young Robert Elwell, who had "put him on" to the Blue Star scheme.

Parvis, at Mary's first startled cry, had thrown her a sobering glance through his impartial glasses.

"Bob Elwell wasn't smart enough, that's all; if he had been, he might have turned round and served Boyne the same way. It's the kind of thing that happens every day in business. I guess it's what the scientists call the survival of the fittest," said Mr. Parvis, evidently pleased with the aptness of his analogy.

Mary felt a physical shrinking from the next question she tried to frame; it was as though the words on her lips had a taste that nauseated her.

"But then—you accuse my husband of doing something dishonorable?"

Mr. Parvis surveyed the question dispassionately. "Oh, no, I don't. I don't even say it wasn't straight." He glanced up and down the long lines of books, as if one of them might have supplied him with the definition he sought. "I don't say it wasn't straight, and yet I don't say it was straight. It was business." After all, no definition in his category could be more comprehensive than that.

Mary sat staring at him with a look of terror. He seemed to her like the indifferent, implacable emissary of some dark, formless power.

"But Mr. Elwell's lawyers apparently did not take your view, since I suppose the suit was withdrawn by their advice."

"Oh, yes, they knew he hadn't a leg to stand on, technically. It was when they advised him to withdraw the suit that he got desperate. You see, he'd borrowed most of the money he lost in the Blue Star, and he was up a tree. That's why he shot himself when they told him he had no show."

The horror was sweeping over Mary in great, deafening waves.

"He shot himself? He killed himself because of that?"

"Well, he didn't kill himself, exactly. He dragged on two months before he died." Parvis emitted the statement as unemotionally as a gramophone grinding out its "record."

"You mean that he tried to kill himself, and failed? And tried again?"

"Oh, he didn't have to try again," said Parvis, grimly.

They sat opposite each other in silence, he swinging his eyeglass thoughtfully about his finger, she, motionless, her arms stretched along her knees in an attitude of rigid tension.

"But if you knew all this," she began at length, hardly able to force her voice above a whisper, "how is it that when I wrote you at the time of my husband's disappearance you said you didn't understand his letter?"

Parvis received this without perceptible discomfiture. "Why, I didn't understand it—strictly speaking. And it wasn't the time to talk about it, if I had. The Elwell business was settled when the suit was withdrawn. Nothing I could have told you would have helped you to find your husband."

Mary continued to scrutinize him. "Then why are you telling me now?"

Still Parvis did not hesitate. "Well, to begin with, I supposed you knew more than you appear to—I mean about the circumstances of Elwell's death. And then people are talking of it now; the whole matter's been raked up again. And I thought, if you didn't know, you ought to."

She remained silent, and he continued: "You see, it's only come out lately what a bad state Elwell's affairs were in. His wife's a proud woman, and she fought on as long as she could, going out to work, and taking sewing at home, when she got too sick—something with the heart, I believe. But she had his bedridden mother to look after, and the children, and she broke down under it, and finally had to ask for help. That attracted attention to the case, and the papers took it up, and a subscription was started. Everybody out there liked Bob Elwell, and most of the prominent names in the place are down on the list, and people began to wonder why—"

Parvis broke off to fumble in an inner pocket. "Here," he continued, "here's an account of the whole thing from the 'Sentinel'—a little sensational, of course. But I guess you'd better look it over."

He held out a newspaper to Mary, who unfolded it slowly, remembering, as she did so, the evening when, in that same room, the perusal of a clipping from the "Sentinel" had first shaken the depths of her security.

As she opened the paper, her eyes, shrinking from the glaring head-lines, "Widow of Boyne's Victim Forced to Appeal for Aid," ran down the column of text to two portraits inserted in it. The first was her husband's, taken from a photograph made the year they had come to England. It was the picture of him that she liked best, the one that stood on the writing-table up-stairs in her bedroom. As the eyes in the photograph met hers, she felt it would be impossible to read what was said of him, and closed her lids with the sharpness of the pain.

"I thought if you felt disposed to put your name down—" she heard Parvis continue.

She opened her eyes with an effort, and they fell on the other portrait. It was that of a youngish man, slightly built, in rough clothes, with features somewhat blurred by the shadow of a projecting hat-brim. Where had she seen that outline before? She stared at it confusedly, her heart hammering in her throat and ears. Then she gave a cry.

"This is the man—the man who came for my husband!"

She heard Parvis start to his feet, and was dimly aware that she had slipped backward into the corner of the sofa, and that he was bending above her in alarm. With an intense effort she straightened herself, and reached out for the paper, which she had dropped.

"It's the man! I should know him anywhere!" she cried in a voice that sounded in her own ears like a scream.

Parvis's voice seemed to come to her from far off, down end-less, fog-muffled windings.

"Mrs. Boyne, you're not very well. Shall I call somebody? Shall I get a glass of water?"

"No, no, no!" She threw herself toward him, her hand fran-tically clenching the newspaper. "I tell you, it's the man! I know him! He spoke to me in the garden!"

Parvis took the journal from her, directing his glasses to the portrait. "It can't be, Mrs. Boyne. It's Robert Elwell."

"Robert Elwell?" Her white stare seemed to travel into space. "Then it was Robert Elwell who came for him."

"Came for Boyne? The day he went away?" Parvis's voice dropped as hers rose. He bent over, laying a fraternal hand on her, as if to coax her gently back into her seat. "Why, Elwell was dead! Don't you remember?"

Mary sat with her eyes fixed on the picture, unconscious of what he was saying.

"Don't you remember Boyne's unfinished letter to me—the one you found on his desk that day? It was written just after he'd heard of Elwell's death." She noticed an odd shake in Parvis's unemotional voice. "Surely you remember that!" he urged her.

Yes, she remembered: that was the profoundest horror of it. Elwell had died the day before her husband's disappearance; and this was Elwell's portrait; and it was the portrait of the man who had spoken to her in the garden. She lifted her head and looked slowly about the library. The library could have borne witness that it was also the portrait of the man who had come in that day to call Boyne from his unfinished letter. Through the misty surgings of her brain she heard the faint boom of half-forgotten words—words spoken by Alida Stair on the lawn at Pangbourne before Boyne and his wife had ever seen the house at Lyng, or had imagined that they might one day live there.

"This was the man who spoke to me," she repeated.

She looked again at Parvis. He was trying to conceal his disturbance under what he imagined to be an expression of indulgent commiseration; but the edges of his lips were blue. "He thinks me mad; but I'm not mad," she reflected; and suddenly there flashed upon her a way of justifying her strange affirmation.

She sat quiet, controlling the quiver of her lips, and waiting till she could trust her voice to keep its habitual level; then she said, looking straight at Parvis: "Will you answer me one question, please? When was it that Robert Elwell tried to kill himself?"

"When—when?" Parvis stammered.

"Yes; the date. Please try to remember."

She saw that he was growing still more afraid of her. "I have a reason," she insisted gently.

"Yes, yes. Only I can't remember. About two months before, I should say."

"I want the date," she repeated.

Parvis picked up the newspaper. "We might see here," he said, still humoring her. He ran his eyes down the page. "Here it is. Last October—the—"

She caught the words from him. "The 20th, wasn't it?" With a sharp look at her, he verified. "Yes, the 20th. Then you did know?"

"I know now." Her white stare continued to travel past him. "Sunday, the 20th—that was the day he came first."

Parvis's voice was almost inaudible. "Came here first?"

"Yes."

"You saw him twice, then?"

"Yes, twice." She breathed it at him with dilated eyes. "He came first on the 20th of October. I remember the date because it was the day we went up Meldon Steep for the first time." She felt a faint gasp of inward laughter at the thought that but for that she might have forgotten.

Parvis continued to scrutinize her, as if trying to intercept her gaze.

"We saw him from the roof," she went on. "He came down the lime avenue toward the house. He was dressed just as he is in that picture. My husband saw him first. He was frightened, and ran down ahead of me; but there was no one there. He had vanished."

"Elwell had vanished?" Parvis faltered.

"Yes." Their two whispers seemed to grope for each other. "I couldn't think what had happened. I see now. He tried to come then; but he wasn't dead enough—he couldn't reach us. He had to wait for two months; and then he came back again—and Ned went with him."

She nodded at Parvis with the look of triumph of a child who has successfully worked out a difficult puzzle. But suddenly she lifted her hands with a desperate gesture, pressing them to her bursting temples.

"Oh, my God! I sent him to Ned—I told him where to go! I sent him to this room!" she screamed out.

She felt the walls of the room rush toward her, like inward falling ruins; and she heard Parvis, a long way off, as if through the ruins, crying to her, and struggling to get at her. But she was numb to his touch, she did not know what he was saying. Through the tumult she heard but one clear note, the voice of Alida Stair, speaking on the lawn at Pangbourne.

"You won't know till afterward," it said. "You won't know till long, long afterward."

ZORA NEALE HURSTON

Zora Neale Hurston lived a mosaic life full of highs and lows played out in small Southern towns and the streets of Harlem where she was sometimes the heart of the party, sometimes an outcast and alone, but always fiercely grounded in her own independent will.

She learned that sense of independence in Eatonville, Florida, one of the first all-black townships where the community lived free of the direct effects of a white-privileged world. The town shaped Hurston's understanding of herself and afforded her what Alice Walker later called "racial health." And yet, as a darker-skinned girl, Hurston felt the perniciousness of oppression even in the idylls of Eatonville. She witnessed (and later wrote about) the consequences of a virulent patriarchy on black women and the poison of a trickled-down racism that still valued lighter skin even among the all-black community.

After years of hardship following her mother's death (and her father's abandonment) when she was thirteen, Hurston lied her way into high school at twenty-six. All she had ever wanted was an education. She got one. She went on to Howard University and then Barnard College where she studied anthropology and started writing stories—which led to her introduction to the major figures of the Harlem Renaissance.

Though quite successful, she never really fit with the over-arching tenets of the other Renaissance writers. Hurston didn't want to write any truth but her own. And her own truth about intraracial prejudice, folk culture and dialects, the sometimes weak, abusive black men and often strong, enduring black women who were comfortable with their own sexuality wasn't the truth her male Renaissance colleagues wanted to hear.

Cut off from the black literary world, Hurston returned to Florida, moving from one menial job to another until she suffered a stroke and died alone and destitute, buried by charity in an unmarked grave. She lay there, forgotten, until Alice Walker found her and gave Hurston back to the world in the hopes that we will take better care of her legacy than we did her life.

Zora Neale Hurston wasn't a dreamer who soared above conventions or a visionary who imagined a life free of oppression. She was a pragmatist and a survivor. She was a woman who endured countless attempts to break her, to cast her aside, to forget her. She resisted those who wanted to silence her. And she compels us to resist and to endure as well.

POKER!

Time: Present

Place: New York

Cast of characters: Nunkie, Too-Sweet, Peckerwood, Black Baby, Sack Daddy, Tush Hawg, Aunt Dilsey

Scene: A shabby front room in a shotgun house.

A door covered by dingy portieres upstage C. Small panel window in side Wall L. Plain centre table with chairs drawn up about it. Gaudy calendars on wall. Battered piano against wall R. Kerosene lamp with reflector against wall on either side of room.

At rise of curtain NUNKIE is at piano playing . . . Others at table with small stacks of chips before each man. TUSH HAWG is seated at table so that he faces audience. He is expertly riffing the cards . . . looks over his shoulder and speaks to NUNKIE.

TUSH HAWG: Come on here, Nunkie—and take a hand! You're holding up the game. You been woofin' round here about the poker you can play—now do it!

NUNKIE: Yeah, I plays poker. I plays the piano and Gawd knows I plays the devil. I'm Uncle Bob with a wooden leg!

BLACK BABY: Aw, you can be had! Come on and get in the game! My britches is cryin' for your money! Come on, don't give the healer no trouble!

NUNKIE: Soon as I play the deck I'm comin' and take you all's money! Don' rush me.

Ace means the first time that I met you.

Duece means there was nobody there but us two.

Trey means the third party—Charlie was his name.

Four spot means the fourth time you tried that same old game—

Five spot means five years you played me for a clown

Six spot means six feet of earth when the deal goes down

Now I'm holding the seven spot for each day of the week

Eight means eight hours that she Sheba-ed with your Sheik—

Nine spot means nine hours that I work hard every day—

Ten spot means tenth of every month I brought you
home my pay—

The Jack is three-card Charlie who played me for
a goat

The Queen, that's my pretty Mama , also trying to
cut my throat—

The King stands for Sweet Papa Nunkie and he's
goin' to wear the crown

So be careful you all ain't broke when the deal
goes down!

(He laughs—X'es to table, bringing piano stool for seat)

TUSH HAWG: Aw now, brother, two dollars for your
seat before you try to sit in this game.

NUNKIE: (Laughs sheepishly—puts money down—
TUSH HAWG pushes stack of chips toward
him. Bus.) I didn't put it down because I knew
you all goin' to be puttin' it right back in my
pocket.

BECKERWOOD: Aw, Y'all go ahead and play. (to
TUSH HAWG) Deal! (TUSH HAWG begins to
deal for draw poker. The game gets tense. SACK
DADDY is first man at TUSH's left—he throws
back three cards and is dealt three more.)

SACK DADDY: My luck sure is rotten! My gal must be

cheatin' on me. I ain't had a pair since John Henry had a hammer!

BLACK BABY: (Drawing three new cards) You might be fooling the rest with the cryin' you're doin' but I'm squattin' for you! You're cryin' worse than cryin' Emma!

TOO-SWEET: (Studying his three new cards) (Sings) When yo' cards gets lucky, oh Partner, you oughter be in a rolin' game.

AUNT DILSEY: (Enters through portieres—stands and looks disapprovingly) You all oughter be ashamed of yourself, gamblin' and carryin' on like this!

BLACK BABY: Aw, this ain't no harm, Aunt Dilsey! You go on back to bed and git your night's rest.

AUNT DILSEY: No harm! I know all about these no-harm sins! If you don't stop this card playin', all of you all goin' to die and go to Hell. (Shakes warning finger—exits through portieres—while she is talking the men have been hiding cards out of their hands and pulling aces out of sleeves and vest pockets and shoes—it is done quickly, one does not see the other do it)

NUNKIE: (Shoving a chip forward) A dollar!

SACK DADDY: Raise you two.

BLACK BABY: I don't like to strain with nobody but

it's goin' to cost you five. Come on, you shag-nags! This hand I got is enough to pull a country man into town.

TOO-SWEET: You all act like you're spuddin'! Bet some money! Put your money where your mouth is.

TUSH HAWG: Twenty-five dollars to keep my company! Dog-gone, I'm spreadin' my knots!

SACK DADDY: And I bet you a fat man I'll take your money—I call you. (Turns up his cards—he has four aces and king)

TUSH HAWG: (Showing his cards) Youse a liar! I ain't dealt you no aces. Don't try to carry the Pam-Pam to me 'cause I'll gently chain-gang for you!

SACK DADDY: Oh yeah! I ain't goin' to fit no jail for you and nobody else. I'm to get me a green club and season it over your head. Then I'll give my case to Miss Bush and let Mother Green stand my bond! I got deal them aces!

NUNKIE: That's a lie! Both of you is lyin'! Lyin' like the cross-ties from New York to Key West! How can you all hold aces when I got four? Somebody is goin' to vest hell before midnight!

BECKERWOOD: If you do dona you woof at Tush Hawg. I'm goin' to bust hell wide open with a man!

BLACK BABY: (Pulls out razor—Bus.) My chop-axe tells me I got the only clean aces they is on this table!

Before I leave you all rob me outa my money, I'm goin' to die it off!

TOO-SWEET: I promised the devil one man and I'm goin' to give him five! (Draws gun)

TUSH HAWG: Don't draw your bosom on me! God sent me a pistol and I'm goin' to send hire a man! (FIRES. Bus. for all)

AUNT DILSEY: (Enters after shooting bus. Stands. Bus. drops to chair.) They wouldn't lissen—(Looks men over—Bus.) It sure is goin' to be a whole lot tougher in hell now!

Curtain

Lawing and Jawing

Time: Present

Place: Way cross Georgia

Scene: Judge Dunfumy's Court.

Persons: Judge Dunfumy, Officer Simpson and another, Jemima Flapcakes, Cliff Mullins, John Barnes, two lawyers, a clerk, a pretty girl and her escort.

Setting: Usual court-room arrangement, except that there is a large red arrow pointing off-stage left, marked "To Jail."

At rise everybody is in place except the Judge. Suddenly the CLERK looks offstage right and motions for everybody to rise. Enter the JUDGE. He wears a black cap and gown and has his gavel in his hand. The two POLICEMEN walk behind him holding up his gown. He mounts the bench and glares all about him before he seats himself. There is a PRETTY GIRL in the front row left, and he takes a good look at her, smiles, frowns at her escort. He motions the police to leave him and take their places with the spectators and he then raps vigorously with his gavel for order.

JUDGE: Hear! Hear! Court is set! My honor is on de bench. You moufy folks set up! (He glares at the boy with the pretty girl) All right, Mr. Whistle-britches, just keep up dat jawing now and see how much time I'll give you!

BOY: I wasn't talking, your honor.

JUDGE: Well, quit looking so moufy. (to CLERK) Call de first case. And I warn each and all dat my honor is in bad humor dis mawnin'. I'd give a canary bird twenty years for peckin' at a elephant. (to CLERK) Bring 'em on.

CLERK: (Reading) Cliff Mullins, charged with assault upon his wife with a weapon and disturbing the peace. (As CLIFF is led to the bar by the officer, the JUDGE glares ferociously at the prisoner. His wife, all bandages, limps up to the bar at the same time.)

JUDGE: So youse one of dese hard-boiled wife-beaters, huh? Just a mean old woman—Jessie! If I don't lay a hearing on you, God's a gopher! Now what made you cut such a caper?

CLIFF: Judge, I didn't go to hunt her. Saturday night I was down on Dearborn Street in a nasty-ditch-buffet flat—

JUDGE: A nasty ditch?

CLIFF: Aw, at Emma Hayles' house.

JUDGE: Oh, yes. Go on.

CLIFF: Well, (Points thumb at wife) she come down dere and claim I took her money and she claimed I wuz spending it on Emma.

CLIFF'S WIFE: Aind dat's just whut he was doing, too, Judge.

CLIFF: Aw, she's tellin' a great big ole Georgia lie, Judge. I wasn't spendin' no money of her'n.

WOMAN: Yes he was, Judge. There wasn't no money for him to git but mine. He ain't hit a lick of work since God been to Macon. Know whut he 'lowed when I worry him 'bout workin'? Says he wouldn't take a job wid de Careless Love Lumber Company, puttin' out whut make you do me lak you do, do, do.

JUDGE: So, you goes for a sweet-back, do you?

CLIIFF: Naw suh, Judge. I'd be glad to work if I could find a job.

JUDGE: How long you been outa work?

CLIFF: Seventeen years—

JUDGE: Seventeen years? (to woman) You been takin' keer of dis man for seventeen years?

WOMAN: Naw, but he been so mean to me, it seems lak seventeen years.

JUDGE: Now you tell me just where he hurt you.

WOMAN: Judge, tell you de truth, I'm hurt all over. (Rubs her buttocks) Fact is I'm cut.

JUDGE: Did you git cut in de fracas?

WOMAN: (Feeling the back of her left thigh below her buttocks) Not in de fracas, Judge—just below it. (She starts to show the JUDGE where she has been cut. He motions to stop her.)

JUDGE: Stop! (to Officer Simpson) Grab him. Put him in de shade.

CLIFF: Judge, I'm unguilty! I ain't laid de weight of my hand on her in malice. You got me 'cused of murder and I ain't harmed a child.

JUDGE: Lemme ast you something. Didn't you know dat all de women in dis town belongs to me? Beat my women and I'll stuff you in jail. 90 years. Take 'im away. (CLIFF is led off to jail. JUDGE looks angrily at the boy who is holding hands with the pretty girl). You runs me hot and I'm just dyin' to sit on yo' case. Whut you in here for?

BOY: Nothin'.

JUDGE: Well, whut you doin' in my court, you gater-faced rascal?

BOY: My girl wanted to see whut was goin' on, so I brought her in.

JUDGE: Oh yeah! (Smiles at GIRL) She was usin' good sense to come see whut I'm doin', but how come you come in here? You gointer have a hard time gittin' out.

BOY: I ain't done a thing. I ain't never done nothin'. I'm just as clean as a fish, and he been in bathin' all his life.

JUDGE: You ain't done nothin', hunh? Well den youse guilty of vacancy. Grab 'im, Simpson, and search 'im—and if he got any concealed weapons, I'm gointer give 'im lifetime and eight years mo'. (The OFFICER seizes the boy and frisks him. All he finds is a new deck of cards. The JUDGE looks at them in triumph.) Uhh hunh! I knowed it, one of dese skin game jelly-beans. Robbin' hard workin' men out they money.

BOY: Judge, I ain't used 'em at all. See, dey's brand new.

JUDGE: Well, den youse charged wid totin' concealed cards and attempt to gamble. Ten years at hard labor. Put him in de dark, Simpson, and throw de key away. (He looks at the girl and beams.) Don't you worry bout how you gointer git home. You gointer be took home right, 'cause I'm gointer take you myself. Bring on de next one, Clerk.

CLERK: Jemima Flap-Cakes, charged with illegal possession and sale of alcoholic liquors.

JUDGE: (She is a fat, black, belligerent looking woman. JUDGE looks coldly at her.) Well, you heard whut he said. Is you guilty or unguilty? And I'm tellin' you right now dat when you come up befo' me it's just like youse in church. You better have a strong determination, and you better tell a good experience.

JEMIMA: (Arms akimbo) Yes, I sold it and I'll sell it again. (snaps fingers and shakes hips) How does ole booze-selling mama talk?

JUDGE: Yes, five thousand dollars and ten years in jail. (Snaps fingers and shakes hips) How does ole heavy fining papa talk? (She is led away, shouting and weeping)

CLERK: De Otis Blunt, charged wid stealint a mule. (LAWYER arises and comes forward with the prisoner)

LAWYER: You can't convict this man. I'm here to represent him.

JUDGE: Yo' mouf might spout lak a coffee pot but I got a lawyer (Looks at other lawyer) dat kin beat yours segastuatin'. (Looks admiring at girl) How am I chewin' my dictionary and minglin' my alphabets?

LAWYER: Well, I kin try, can't I?

JUDGE: Oh yeah, you kin try, but I kin see right now where he's gointer git all de time dat God ever made dat ain't been used already. From now on. (To LAWYER) Go 'head, and spread yo' lungs all over Georgy, but he's goin' to jail.' Mules must be respected.

LAWYER: (Striking a pose at the bar) Your Honor, (Looks at the pretty girl) Ladies and Gentlemen—

JUDGE: Never mind bout dat lady. You talk yo' chat to me.

LAWYER: This is a clear case of syllogism! Again I say syllogism. My client is innocent because it was a dark night when they say he stole the mule and that's against all laws of syllogism. (JUDGE looks impressed and laughs)

JUDGE: Dat ole fool do know somethin' 'bout law.

LAWYER: When George Washington was pleading de case of Marbury vs. Madison, what did he say? What did he say? Scintillate, scintillate, Globule orific. Fain would I fathom thy nature's specific. Loftily poised in ether capacious, strongly resembling a gem carbonacious. What did Abraham Lincoln say about mule-stealing? When torrid Phoebut refuses his presence and ceases to lamp with fierce incandescence, then you illumine the regions supernal, scintillate, scintillate, semper nocturnal. Syllogism, again I say syllogism. (He takes his seat amid applause)

JUDGE: Man, youse a pleadin' fool. You knows yo' rules and by-laws.

OTHER LAWYER: Let me show my glory. Let me spread my habeas corpus.

JUDGE: 'Tain't no use. Dis lawyer done convinced me.

OTHER LAWYER: But, lemme parade my material—

JUDGE: Parade yo' material anywhere you wants to exceptin' befo' me. Dis lil girl wants to go home and I'm goin' with her and enjoy de consequences. Court's adjourned.

CURTAIN

VIRGINIA WOOLF

*N*o gathering of women who wrote would be complete without Virginia Woolf. Like many of the writers here, she most certainly, defiantly, transcendently wrote—stories, novels, essays. But Woolf also took up the fight for women's rights and women writing and carried it out into the world by way of lectures, letters, and essays and through starting her own printing house and publishing the books no one else would. She stepped up to the stagnant English patriarchy and gave it a well-deserved wake-up slap across the cheek.

By the time she reached adulthood and independence after the death of her father, Woolf had had enough of being tethered and silenced. Born into the blended family of two widowers with eight children, Woolf and her sisters were habitually overlooked—refused the education their brothers received, invisible to their self-indulgent father, and an afterthought to their mother who was spread thin caring for the boys and nursing sick relatives. The neglect had privileges—Woolf read freely from her father's extensive library—but it also came at a terrible cost. Both Vanessa and Virginia later accused their older half-brothers of sexual abuse that lasted from young childhood until the women had a home of their own.

This chronic abuse likely contributed to the other demon haunting Woolf's life—a recurring battle with severe mental illness. At times, the illness ravaged her, leading to suicide attempts and months of institutionalization, but Woolf was more than her mental illness. She was a stalwart survivor, a vibrant soul who lived intensely, gathering the world's energy and channeling it into her work, which vibrates with that same expectant watching. There lingers still an assumption of the fragility of her mind, but what a warrior Woolf must have been to battle for fifty years against a relentless internal attack on her reason. She won more than she lost, and we are all the richer for it—for those times when she used her words to hold the chaos at bay and showed us new ways to see the world, new ways to see ourselves.

Virginia Woolf wrote to save her life. She wrote to save ours.

Kew Gardens

*F*rom the oval-shaped flower-bed there rose perhaps a hundred stalks spreading into heart-shaped or tongue-shaped leaves half way up and unfurling at the tip red or blue or yellow petals marked with spots of colour raised upon the surface; and from the red, blue or yellow gloom of the throat emerged a straight bar, rough with gold dust and slightly clubbed at the end. The petals were voluminous enough to be stirred by the summer breeze, and when they moved, the red, blue and yellow lights passed one over the other, staining an inch of the brown earth beneath with a spot of the most intricate colour. The light fell either upon the smooth, grey back of a pebble, or, the shell of a snail with its brown, circular veins, or falling into a raindrop, it expanded with such intensity of red, blue and yellow the thin walls of water that one expected them to burst and disappear. Instead, the drop was left in a second silver grey once more, and the light now settled upon the flesh of a leaf, revealing the branching thread of fibre beneath the surface, and again it moved on and spread its illumination in the vast green spaces beneath the dome of the heart-shaped and tongue-shaped leaves. Then the breeze stirred rather more briskly overhead and the colour was flashed into the air above, into the eyes of the men and women who walk in Kew Gardens in July.

The figures of these men and women straggled past the flower-bed with a curiously irregular movement not unlike that of the white and blue butterflies who crossed the turf in zig-zag flights from bed to bed. The man was about six inches in front of the woman, strolling carelessly, while she bore on with greater purpose, only turning her head now and then to see that the children were not too far behind. The man kept this distance in front of the woman purposely, though perhaps unconsciously, for he wished to go on with his thoughts.

"Fifteen years ago I came here with Lily," he thought. "We sat somewhere over there by a lake and I begged her to marry me all through the hot afternoon. How the dragonfly kept circling round us: how clearly I see the dragonfly and her shoe with the square silver buckle at the toe. All the time I spoke I saw her shoe and when it moved impatiently I knew without looking up what she was going to say: the whole of her seemed to be in her shoe. And my love, my desire, were in the dragonfly; for some reason I thought that if it settled there, on that leaf, the broad one with the red flower in the middle of it, if the dragonfly settled on the leaf she would say 'Yes' at once. But the dragonfly went round and round: it never settled anywhere—of course not, happily not, or I shouldn't be walking here with Eleanor and the children— Tell me, Eleanor. D'you ever think of the past?"

"Why do you ask, Simon?"

"Because I've been thinking of the past. I've been thinking of Lily, the woman I might have married. . . . Well, why are you silent? Do you mind my thinking of the past?"

"Why should I mind, Simon? Doesn't one always think of the past, in a garden with men and women lying under the trees? Aren't they one's past, all that remains of it, those men and women, those ghosts lying under the trees, . . . one's happiness, one's reality?"

"For me, a square silver shoe buckle and a dragonfly—"

"For me, a kiss. Imagine six little girls sitting before their easels twenty years ago, down by the side of a lake, painting the water-lilies, the first red water-lilies I'd ever seen. And suddenly a kiss, there on the back of my neck. And my hand shook all the afternoon so that I couldn't paint. I took out my watch and marked the hour when I would allow myself to think of the kiss for five minutes only—it was so precious—the kiss of an old grey-haired woman with a wart on her nose, the mother of all my kisses all my life. Come, Caroline, come, Hubert."

They walked on past the flower-bed, now walking four abreast, and soon diminished in size among the trees and looked half transparent as the sunlight and shade swam over their backs in large trembling irregular patches.

In the oval flower bed the snail, whose shell had been stained red, blue, and yellow for the space of two minutes or so, now appeared to be moving very slightly in its shell, and next began to labour over the crumbs of loose earth which broke away and rolled down as it passed over them. It appeared to have a definite goal in front of it, differing in this respect from the singular high stepping angular green insect who attempted to cross in front of it, and waited for a second with its antennæ trembling as if in deliberation, and then stepped off as rapidly and strangely in the opposite direction. Brown cliffs with deep green lakes in the hollows, flat, blade-like trees that waved from root to tip, round boulders of grey stone, vast crumpled surfaces of a thin crackling texture—all these objects lay across the snail's progress between one stalk and another to his goal. Before he had decided whether to circumvent the arched tent of a dead leaf or to breast it there came past the bed the feet of other human beings.

This time they were both men. The younger of the two wore an expression of perhaps unnatural calm; he raised his eyes and fixed them very steadily in front of him while his companion spoke, and directly his companion had done speaking he looked on the ground again and sometimes opened his lips only after a long pause and sometimes did not open them at all. The elder man had a curiously uneven and shaky method of walking, jerking his hand forward and throwing up his head abruptly, rather in the manner of an impatient carriage horse tired of waiting outside a house; but in the man these gestures were irresolute and pointless. He talked almost incessantly; he smiled to himself and again began to talk, as if the smile had been an answer. He was talking about spirits—the spirits of the dead, who, according to him, were even now telling him all sorts of odd things about their experiences in Heaven.

"Heaven was known to the ancients as Thessaly, William, and now, with this war, the spirit matter is rolling between the hills like thunder." He paused, seemed to listen, smiled, jerked his head and continued:—

"You have a small electric battery and a piece of rubber to insulate the wire—isolate?—insulate?—well, we'll skip the details, no good going into details that wouldn't be understood— and in short the little machine stands in any convenient position by the head of the bed, we will say, on a neat mahogany stand. All arrangements being properly fixed by workmen under my direction, the widow applies her ear and summons the spirit by sign as agreed. Women! Widows! Women in black—"

Here he seemed to have caught sight of a woman's dress in the distance, which in the shade looked a purple black. He took off his hat, placed his hand upon his heart, and hurried towards her muttering and gesticulating feverishly. But William caught him by the sleeve and touched a flower with the tip of his walking-stick in order to divert the old man's attention. After looking at it for a moment in some confusion the old man bent his ear to it and seemed to answer a voice speaking from it, for he began talking about the forests of Uruguay which he had visited hundreds of years ago in company with the most beautiful young woman in Europe. He could be heard murmuring about forests of Uruguay blanketed with the wax petals of tropical roses, nightingales, sea beaches, mermaids, and women drowned at sea, as he suffered himself to be moved on by William, upon whose face the look of stoical patience grew slowly deeper and deeper.

Following his steps so closely as to be slightly puzzled by his gestures came two elderly women of the lower middle class, one stout and ponderous, the other rosy cheeked and nimble. Like most people of their station they were frankly fascinated by any signs of eccentricity betokening a disordered brain, especially in the well-to-do; but they were too far off to be certain whether the gestures were merely eccentric or genuinely mad. After they had scrutinised the old man's back in silence for a moment and given each other a queer, sly look, they went on energetically piecing together their very complicated dialogue:

"Nell, Bert, Lot, Cess, Phil, Pa, he says, I says, she says, I says, I says, I says—"

"My Bert, Sis, Bill, Grandad, the old man, sugar,

Sugar, flour, kippers, greens,

Sugar, sugar, sugar."

The ponderous woman looked through the pattern of falling words at the flowers standing cool, firm, and upright in the earth, with a curious expression. She saw them as a sleeper waking from a heavy sleep sees a brass candlestick reflecting the light in an unfamiliar way, and closes his eyes and opens them, and seeing the brass candlestick again, finally starts broad awake and stares at the candlestick with all his powers. So the heavy woman came to a standstill opposite the oval-shaped flower bed, and ceased even to pretend to listen to what the other woman was saying. She stood there letting the words fall over her, swaying the top part of her body slowly backwards and forwards, looking at the flowers. Then she suggested that they should find a seat and have their tea.

The snail had now considered every possible method of reaching his goal without going round the dead leaf or climbing over it. Let alone the effort needed for climbing a leaf, he was doubtful whether the thin texture which vibrated with such an alarming crackle when touched even by the tip of his horns would bear his weight; and this determined him finally to creep beneath it, for there was a point where the leaf curved high enough from the ground to admit him. He had just inserted his head in the opening and was taking stock of the high brown roof and was getting used to the cool brown light when two other people came past outside on the turf. This time they were both young, a young man and a young woman. They were both in the prime of youth, or even in that season which precedes the prime of youth, the season before the smooth pink folds of the flower have burst their gummy case, when the wings of the butterfly, though fully grown, are motionless in the sun.

"Lucky it isn't Friday," he observed.

"Why? D'you believe in luck?"

"They make you pay sixpence on Friday."

"What's sixpence anyway? Isn't it worth sixpence?"

"What's 'it'—what do you mean by 'it'?"

"O, anything—I mean—you know what I mean."

Long pauses came between each of these remarks; they were uttered in toneless and monotonous voices. The couple stood still on the edge of the flower bed, and together pressed the end of her parasol deep down into the soft earth. The action and the fact that his hand rested on the top of hers expressed their feelings in a strange way, as these short insignificant words also expressed something, words with short wings for their heavy body of meaning, inadequate to carry them far and thus alighting awkwardly upon the very common objects that surrounded them, and were to their inexperienced touch so massive; but who knows (so they thought as they pressed the parasol into the earth) what precipices aren't concealed in them, or what slopes of ice don't shine in the sun on the other side? Who knows? Who has ever seen this before? Even when she wondered what sort of tea they gave you at Kew, he felt that something loomed up behind her words, and stood vast and solid behind them; and the mist very slowly rose and uncovered—O, Heavens, what were those shapes?—little white tables, and waitresses who looked first at her and then at him; and there was a bill that he would pay with a real two shilling piece, and it was real, all real, he assured himself, fingering the coin in his pocket, real to everyone except to him and to her; even to him it began to seem real; and then—but it was too exciting to stand and think any longer, and he pulled the parasol out of the earth with a jerk and was impatient to find the place where one had tea with other people, like other people.

"Come along, Trissie; it's time we had our tea."

"Wherever *does* one have one's tea?" she asked with the oddest thrill of excitement in her voice, looking vaguely round and letting herself be drawn on down the grass path, trailing her parasol, turning her head this way and that way, forgetting her tea, wishing to go down there and then down there, remembering orchids and cranes among wild flowers, a Chinese pagoda and a crimson crested bird; but he bore her on.

Thus one couple after another with much the same irregular and aimless movement passed the flower-bed and were enveloped in layer after layer of green blue vapour, in which at first their bodies had substance and a dash of colour, but later both substance and colour dissolved in the green-blue atmosphere. How hot it was! So hot that even the thrush chose to hop, like a mechanical bird, in the shadow of the flowers, with long pauses between one movement and the next; instead of rambling vaguely the white butterflies danced one above another, making with their white shifting flakes the outline of a shattered marble column above the tallest flowers; the glass roofs of the palm house shone as if a whole market full of shiny green umbrellas had opened in the sun; and in the drone of the aeroplane the voice of the summer sky murmured its fierce soul. Yellow and black, pink and snow white, shapes of all these colours, men, women, and children were spotted for a second upon the horizon, and then, seeing the breadth of yellow that lay upon the grass, they wavered and sought shade beneath the trees, dissolving like drops of water in the yellow and green atmosphere, staining it faintly with red and blue. It seemed as if all gross and heavy bodies had sunk down in the heat motionless and lay huddled upon the ground, but their voices went wavering from them as if they were flames lolling from the thick waxen bodies of candles. Voices. Yes, voices. Wordless voices, breaking the silence suddenly with such depth of contentment, such passion of desire, or, in the voices of children, such freshness of surprise; breaking the silence? But there was no silence; all the time the motor omnibuses were turning their wheels and changing their gear; like a vast nest of Chinese boxes all of wrought steel turning ceaselessly one within another the city murmured; on the top of which the voices cried aloud and the petals of myriads of flowers flashed their colours into the air.

POEMS

Emily Dickinson

*M*any people find Emily Dickinson confounding—as a poet, as a person, during her life and after her death. She left many tantalizingly loose threads in her poems and her letters, and scholars have continued to pull at those threads, weaving them into one crafted context or another, all for the purpose of unraveling the enigma of Emily Dickinson. All for the purpose of defining her—privileged girl, neglected child, lovesick, heartbroken, lover of men or women, haughty recluse, ill and isolated, lonely, contented. But at every turn, Emily Dickinson thwarts those imposed definitions—both then and now. She could be all of those things or none of them.

In her life, Emily Dickinson intentionally unmoored herself from the expectations of her society. Deeply spiritual, she rejected the hellfire-and-brimstone religion that was forced on her community and, instead, opted to find God in the beauty and grace of the natural world around her. At about the same time, when she was in her twenties, Dickinson began to turn her back on the imposed social obligations for women of her time. She did not go "calling" on her neighbors, and she often excused herself when others came to visit the Dickinson house. And yet, she routinely interacted with the children in Amherst, indulging them with baskets of goodies and a listening ear, encouraging them to "never 'improve,'" but rather to stay as they were—wild and free. She maintained robust relationships with the people closest to her and extensive correspondence with more far-flung friends. She wasn't withdrawing from the world out of fear or bitterness like a recluse. Dickinson simply chose "her own Society."

Likewise, in her poetry, Dickinson pursues her own course with absolute disdain for the accepted, male-curated conventions of the time. She capitalizes and punctuates as she sees fit to convey emphasis and meaning in her poems. Her slant rhyme is both relevant to the content of her work and consistent with her resistance to fulfilling expectation—just a little off from what we think we want but surprisingly satisfying all the same. She writes out of the liberation she has claimed for herself. No subject taboo, no form sacrosanct, no titles for her poems even as she rejected them for herself.

Emily Dickinson might be confounding, indeed, though not like a puzzle to be solved or a problem to be fixed, but rather like a Jackson Pollack or the expanse of a starry night—astonishing, too much to comprehend all at once, ever changing, awe inspiring, yet speaking to us in plain, powerful ways. The reader must come to Dickinson, both the woman and the writer, without expectation to see what's there rather than to try to fill in the blanks—because Dickinson leaves the gaps, literal and figurative, on purpose. She makes space for all of us to imagine the possible beyond boundaries, to play, to grow, to decide for ourselves who we are and who we want to be.

A Bird Came Down

the Walk

A Bird came down the Walk—
He did not know I saw—
He bit an Angleworm in halves
And ate the fellow, raw,

And then he drank a Dew
From a convenient Grass—
And then hopped sidewise to the Wall
To let a Beetle pass—

He glanced with rapid eyes,
That hurried all around—
They looked like frightened Beads, I thought—
He stirred his Velvet Head

Like one in danger, Cautious,
I offered him a Crumb
And he unrolled his feathers
And rowed him softer home—

Than Oars divide the Ocean,
Too silver for a seam—
Or Butterflies, off Banks of Noon
Leap, plashless as they swim.

Hope Is the Thing
with Feathers

Hope is the thing with feathers
That perches in the soul,
And sings the tune without the words,
And never stops at all,

And sweetest in the gale is heard;
And sore must be the storm
That could abash the little bird
That kept so many warm.

I've heard it in the chillest land,
And on the strangest sea;
Yet, never, in extremity,
It asked a crumb of me.

A Man May Make

a Remark

A Man may make a Remark—
In itself—a quiet thing
That may furnish the Fuse unto a Spark
In dormant nature—lain—

Let us divide—with skill—
Let us discourse—with care—
Powder exists in Charcoal—
Before it exists in Fire—

Wild Nights—
Wild Nights!

Wild nights—Wild nights!
Were I with thee
Wild Nights should be
Our luxury!

Futile—the winds—
To a heart in port—
Done with the compass—
Done with the chart!

Rowing in Eden—
Ah—the sea!
Might I but moor—Tonight—
In thee!

It's All I Have to Bring Today

It's all I have to bring today—
This, and my heart beside—
This, and my heart, and all the fields—
And all the meadows wide—
Be sure you count—should I forget
Some one the sum could tell—
This, and my heart, and all the Bees
Which in the Clover dwell.

GERTRUDE STEIN

*g*ertrude Stein's fingerprints dance across much of the Modernist landscape—a fact she was happy to tout for herself in *Everybody's Autobiography*: "I have been the creative literary mind of the century." While the singularity of her boast might be questionable, there is no argument that Stein buoyed, shaped, and opened doors for nearly all of the literary giants of her age, not to mention the artistic greats: Matisse, Cézanne, and Picasso. Stein is what we would call an "influencer" today, but she was also a writer herself—of novels, poems, plays, and even a few librettos.

Stein ventured early into exploring the relationship between consciousness and writing—a result of her study of psychology with William James at Radcliffe. He introduced her to the ideas that led to the development of "stream of consciousness" as a writing technique and, later, to her own concept of the "continuous present" (the idea that past, present, and future can be conveyed in the present moment). Though deemed "brilliant" by her mentors, Stein found the male-dominated realm of higher education forbidding and stifling and so followed her brother, Leo, to Paris, which would become her forever home.

Shortly after arriving, she was introduced to the other major influence on her artistic perspective—cubism. The works of Cézanne and Picasso particularly, which presented multiple viewpoints of a singular object, abstracted and constructed to imply three-dimensional depth on a two-dimensional canvas, made a perfect visual representation of the ideas with which Stein had long been playing. She began to try to capture the same effect in her writing. It was also here, in Paris, that Stein met the final force that shaped the rest of her destiny: Alice B. Toklas, her partner in life and in writing (Toklas typed and tweaked Stein's work).

In addition to being a patron and a writer, Stein was very much a woman searching for a place in the patriarchal world to be herself—to be as brilliant and witty and ambitious and bombastic as she pleased—and much of her writing comes from her struggle to free herself from words (and meanings) defined by men so that she might speak with her own voice.

GUILLAUME APOLLINAIRE

Give known or pin ware.

Fancy teeth, gas strips.

Elbow elect, sour stout pore, pore caesar, pour state at.

Leave eye lessons I. Leave I. Lessons. I. Leave I

    lessons, I.

A Long Dress

(*Tender Buttons*)

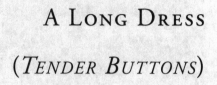

*T*hat is the current that makes machinery, that makes it crackle, what is the current that presents a long line and a necessary waist. What is this current.

What is the wind, what is it.

Where is the serene length, it is there and a dark place is not a dark place, only a white and red are black, only a yellow and green are blue, a pink is scarlet, a bow is every color. A line distinguishes it. A line just distinguishes it.

A Plate (*Tender Buttons*)

*A*n occasion for a plate, an occasional resource is in buying and how soon does washing enable a selection of the same thing neater. If the party is small a clever song is in order.

Plates and a dinner set of colored china. Pack together a string and enough with it to protect the centre, cause a considerable haste and gather more as it is cooling, collect more trembling and not any even trembling, cause a whole thing to be a church.

A sad size a size that is not sad is blue as every bit of blue is precocious. A kind of green a game in green and nothing flat nothing quite flat and more round, nothing a particular color strangely, nothing breaking the losing of no little piece.

A splendid address a really splendid address is not shown by giving a flower freely, it is not shown by a mark or by wetting.

Cut cut in white, cut in white so lately. Cut more than any

other and show it. Show it in the stem and in starting and in evening coming complication.

A lamp is not the only sign of glass. The lamp and the cake are not the only sign of stone. The lamp and the cake and the cover are not the only necessity altogether.

A plan a hearty plan, a compressed disease and no coffee, not even a card or a change to incline each way, a plan that has that excess and that break is the one that shows filling.

A Light in the Moon

(*Tender Buttons*)

A light in the moon the only light is on Sunday. What was the sensible decision. The sensible decision was that notwithstanding many declarations and more music, not even notwithstanding the choice and a torch and a collection, notwithstanding the celebrating hat and a vacation and even more noise than cutting, notwithstanding Europe and Asia and being overbearing, not even notwithstanding an elephant and a strict occasion, not even withstanding more cultivation and some seasoning, not even with drowning and with the ocean being encircling, not even with more likeness and any cloud, not even with terrific sacrifice of pedestrianism and a special resolution, not even more likely to be pleasing. The care with which the rain is wrong and the green is wrong and the white is wrong, the care with which there is a chair and plenty of breathing. The care with which there is incredible justice and likeness, all this makes a magnificent asparagus, and also a fountain.

CHARLOTTE BRONTË

*Y*our land is neither savage nor wild enough," Jane Eyre answers when Mr. Rochester accuses her of being an elf come to bewitch him. So, too, was the world for Jane's creator, Charlotte Brontë, "neither savage nor wild enough." Brontë struggled to make room for herself in a culture that positioned pretty, moneyed women to become wives and mothers, and plain, poor ones to become governesses. Both Brontë and her characters sojourn into the constraints of the sexist, classist society, at times sacrificing their pride in an effort to gain their independence. The characters often benefit from some turn of luck or the hand of God and become heiresses or find love and marriage against all odds, but Brontë won the battle to live life on her own terms with the power of her pen and the brilliance of her talent.

Born the third of six children to a clergyman father too

absorbed in his own work to take notice of any but the sole boy, and to a mother who died when the children were all very young, Charlotte Brontë claimed a freedom rarely offered to girls at the time. Except for a short stint at a nearby school (the inspiration for the bleak Lowood school in *Jane Eyre*) that turned tragic when her eldest sisters died, Charlotte's early years were filled with the fantastic imaginings of the sharp, adventurous minds of the Brontë children as they ran wild over the Yorkshire moors and shaped imaginary worlds in which anything was possible.

Despite the initial efforts after her death to sanctify her, to paint her as a virtuous, compliant, delicate soul, Charlotte Brontë's own fiery, defiant voice rings out in her letters where she condemns the treatment of herself and other governesses at the hands of haughty, entitled employers. She writes of the draining work of teaching "fat-headed oafs" and depicts the joyful, liberated hours at the end of the day as her salvation when her creativity fires, and she escapes, once more, into worlds of her own making.

Charlotte Brontë ventured forth into the suffocating patriarchal world and stood stalwart against its persecutions, gathering the pain and longing she endured and bringing it all home to the wild moors where she was free to transform the savagery of the world into bewitching stories where women are full of desire and ambition, freed from their cages so they can "soar cloud-high."

LIFE

Life, believe, is not a dream
So dark as sages say;
Oft a little morning rain
Foretells a pleasant day.
Sometimes there are clouds of gloom,
But these are transient all;
If the shower will make the roses bloom,
O why lament its fall?
Rapidly, merrily,
Life's sunny hours flit by,
Gratefully, cheerily,
Enjoy them as they fly!
What though Death at times steps in
And calls our Best away?
What though sorrow seems to win,

O'er hope, a heavy sway?

Yet hope again elastic springs,

Unconquered, though she fell;

Still buoyant are her golden wings,

Still strong to bear us well.

Manfully, fearlessly,

The day of trial bear,

For gloriously, victoriously,

Can courage quell despair!

Evening Solace

The human heart has hidden treasures,
In secret kept, in silence sealed—
The thoughts, the hopes, the dreams, the pleasures,
Whose charms were broken if revealed.
And days may pass in gay confusion,
And nights in rosy riot fly,
While, lost in Fame's or Wealth's illusion,
The memory of the Past may die.

But there are hours of lonely musing,
Such as in evening silence come,
When, soft as birds their pinions closing,
The heart's best feelings gather home.
Then in our souls there seems to languish
A tender grief that is not woe;

And thoughts that once wrung groans of anguish,
Now cause but some mild tears to flow.

And feelings, once as strong as passions,
Float softly back—a faded dream;
Our own sharp griefs and wild sensations,
The tale of others' sufferings seem.
Oh! when the heart is freshly bleeding,
How longs it for that time to be,
When, through the mist of years receding,
Its woes but live in reverie!

And it can dwell on moonlight glimmer,
On evening shade and loneliness;
And, while the sky grows dim and dimmer,
Feel no untold and strange distress—
Only a deeper impulse given
By lonely hour and darkened room,
To solemn thoughts that soar to heaven
Seeking a life and world to come.

PASSION

Some have won a wild delight,
By daring wilder sorrow;
Could I gain thy love to-night,
I'd hazard death to-morrow.

Could the battle-struggle earn
One kind glance from thine eye,
How this withering heart would burn,
The heady fight to try!

Welcome nights of broken sleep,
And days of carnage cold,
Could I deem that thou wouldst weep
To hear my perils told.

Tell me, if with wandering bands
I roam full far away,
Wilt thou, to those distant lands,
In spirit ever stray?

Wild, long, a trumpet sounds afar;
Bid me—bid me go
Where Seik and Briton meet in war,
On Indian Sutlej's flow.

Blood has dyed the Sutlej's waves
With scarlet stain, I know;
Indus' borders yawn with graves,
Yet, command me go!

Though rank and high the holocaust
Of nations, steams to heaven,
Glad I'd join the death-doomed host,
Were but the mandate given.

Passion's strength should nerve my arm,
Its ardour stir my life,
Till human force to that dread charm
Should yield and sink in wild alarm,
Like trees to tempest-strife.

If, hot from war, I seek thy love,
Darest thou turn aside?
Darest thou, then, my fire reprove,
By scorn, and maddening pride?

No—my will shall yet control
Thy will, so high and free,
And love shall tame that haughty soul—
Yes—tenderest love for me.

I'll read my triumph in thine eyes,
Behold, and prove the change;
Then leave, perchance, my noble prize,
Once more in arms to range.

I'd die when all the foam is up,
The bright wine sparkling high;
Nor wait till in the exhausted cup
Life's dull dregs only lie.

Then Love thus crowned with sweet reward,
Hope blest with fulness large,
I'd mount the saddle, draw the sword,
And perish in the charge!

EMILY BRONTË

"She should have been a man," wrote Constantin Héger of Emily Brontë. The tall, thin, and by all accounts antisocial young woman left a marked impression on Héger in the few months she (and her sister, Charlotte) attended his academy in Brussels. Héger raved about Emily's keen intellect, her ability to reason and to argue, and he seemed almost intimidated by the fierceness of her will. He clearly admired her, but apparently hardly anyone *liked* Emily Brontë—a sentiment she reciprocated and that bothered her not a whit.

The few crafted, posthumous depictions we have of Emily Brontë sketch a portrait of a young woman socially awkward and shy and so uncomfortable in the world that she rarely left her Yorkshire home—a person as wild and inhospitable as the moors she loved. And yet, much evidence discovered later in letters and journals supports Héger's understanding of her as a woman not shy or reclusive, but abundant in the self-confidence and independent will more expected (and accepted) of a man at the time.

Brontë was most assuredly taciturn, though not from shyness or inadequacy, but rather as a consequence of a devil-may-care disdain for the expected feminine social behaviors that ruled the day. She spoke freely with her family, she engaged with Héger as an equal, she boldly told her students (in her brief stint as a teacher) that she preferred the dog to them, and yet she befriended at least one lonely fellow student in Brussels who called Emily kindhearted. Emily Brontë could be tender or abrupt or aloof as *she* deemed fit. She simply didn't care what people thought of her. She left home when it suited her—to expand her learning and knowledge of the world. And, when it was clear that that world refused to make room for a woman of her temperament and talent, she came back to the isolation of the moors, where she ruled her domain, cared for the wayward animals she rescued in the wilds, and built her own worlds through the creative workings of her own mind.

While Emily Brontë might have appreciated Héger's regard for her intellectual abilities, his assertion that she should have been born a man would have infuriated the fiery spirit who would not bow to society's expectations, declaring instead, "I wish to be as God made me."

Stanzas

Often rebuked, yet always back returning
    To those first feelings that were born with me,
And leaving busy chase of wealth and learning
    For idle dreams of things that cannot be:

To-day, I will seek not the shadowy region;
    Its unsustaining vastness waxes drear;
And visions rising, legion after legion,
    Bring the unreal world too strangely near.

I'll walk, but not in old heroic traces,
    And not in paths of high morality,
And not among the half-distinguished faces,
    The clouded forms of long-past history.

I'll walk where my own nature would be leading:
    It vexes me to choose another guide:
Where the gray flocks in ferny glens are feeding;
    Where the wild wind blows on the mountain side.

What have those lonely mountains worth revealing?
    More glory and more grief than I can tell:
The earth that wakes *one* human heart to feeling
    Can centre both the worlds of Heaven and Hell.

Hope

Hope was but a timid friend;
She sat without the grated den,
Watching how my fate would tend,
Even as selfish-hearted men.

She was cruel in her fear;
Through the bars, one dreary day,
I looked out to see her there,
And she turned her face away!

Like a false guard, false watch keeping,
Still, in strife, she whispered peace;
She would sing while I was weeping;
If I listened, she would cease.

False she was, and unrelenting;
When my last joys strewed the ground,
Even Sorrow saw, repenting,
Those sad relics scattered round;

Hope, whose whisper would have given
Balm to all my frenzied pain,
Stretched her wings, and soared to heaven,
Went, and ne'er returned again!

REMEMBRANCE

Cold in the earth—and the deep snow piled
    above thee,
Far, far removed, cold in the dreary grave!
Have I forgot, my only Love, to love thee,
Severed at last by Time's all-severing wave?

Now, when alone, do my thoughts no longer hover
Over the mountains, on that northern shore,
Resting their wings where heath and fern leaves cover
Thy noble heart forever, ever more?

Cold in the earth—and fifteen wild Decembers,
From those brown hills, have melted into spring;
Faithful, indeed, is the spirit that remembers
After such years of change and suffering!

Sweet Love of youth, forgive, if I forget thee,
While the world's tide is bearing me along;
Other desires and other hopes beset me,
Hopes which obscure, but cannot do thee wrong!

No later light has lightened up my heaven,
No second morn has ever shone for me;
All my life's bliss from thy dear life was given,
All my life's bliss is in the grave with thee.

But, when the days of golden dreams had perished,
And even Despair was powerless to destroy,
Then did I learn how existence could be cherished,
Strengthened, and fed without the aid of joy.

Then did I check the tears of useless passion—
Weaned my young soul from yearning after thine;
Sternly denied its burning wish to hasten
Down to that tomb already more than mine.

And, even yet, I dare not let it languish,
Dare not indulge in memory's rapturous pain;
Once drinking deep of that divinest anguish,
How could I seek the empty world again?

Spellbound

The night is darkening round me,
The wild winds coldly blow;
But a tyrant spell has bound me
And I cannot, cannot go.

The giant trees are bending
Their bare boughs weighed with snow.
And the storm is fast descending,
And yet I cannot go.

Clouds beyond clouds above me,
Wastes beyond wastes below;
But nothing drear can move me;
I will not, cannot go.

FRANCES ELLEN WATKINS HARPER

*F*rances Ellen Watkins Harper was a visionary—both as a literary figure and as a political activist. Born into an uncommon life as a free black woman in Maryland in 1825 with access to a formal education at her uncle's school, Harper's lifelong fight against injustice centered on the common cause of liberty and equality: "We are all bound up together in one great bundle of humanity, and society cannot trample on the weakest and feeblest of its members without receiving the curse in its own soul." An eloquent speaker, she was popular on the abolitionist tour before the Civil War and in high demand addressing suffrage and women's rights groups afterward. With an eerily prophetic clarion call, she spoke to the intersectionality of oppression—how the plight of people of color is woven into the plight of women is woven into the plight of the poor. And as a deeply religious person, she called out the hypocrisy of Christians using interpretations of the Bible to justify racism and sexism. Harper used the power of her education and the beauty of her words to deliver the hard truths her audiences needed to hear.

Much of Harper's literary work (eleven books of poetry, four novels, several short stories, essays, and speeches) also exposes the cruelty of a culture built on slavery and the capriciousness of a society with one set of laws for men and another for women. Her poems are almost all ballads designed to take the reader into an experience, to engage their empathies, to make the reader complicit and thereby to challenge their preconceptions. Likewise, her novels break literary ground in their use of dialect and vernacular, which Harper uses in contrast with deeply complex characters and intricate plots.

That Frances Ellen Watkins Harper is a lesser-known name than most collected here testifies to the power of a white, patriarchal culture to shape its own narrative by deciding who is heard and who is not. That she is included here now is a testament, in part, to the good and necessary work of scholars culling through discarded texts to recover the writings of women and people of color in order to restore them to their rightful place in the literary canon. Harper claims this high place among American literary giants through her own merits as a writer, separate and apart from her astounding work as an activist. She uses her powerful, compelling authorial voice to take us out of our own skins, out of our experiences and into another. She puts us back again, empowered to measure our own souls.

Bible Defense of Slavery

Take sackcloth of the darkest dye,
    And shroud the pulpits round!
Servants of Him that cannot lie,
    Sit mourning on the ground.

Let holy horror blanch each cheek,
    Pale every brow with fears;
And rocks and stones, if ye could speak,
    Ye well might melt to tears!

Let sorrow breathe in every tone,
    In every strain ye raise;
Insult not God's majestic throne
    With th' mockery of praise.

A "reverend" man, whose light should be
    The guide of age and youth,
Brings to the shrine of Slavery
    The sacrifice of truth!

For the direst wrong by man imposed,
    Since Sodom's fearful cry,
The word of life has been unclos'd,
    To give your God the lie.

Oh! When ye pray for heathen lands,
    And plead for their dark shores,
Remember Slavery's cruel hands
    Make heathens at your doors!

A Double Standard

When the gates of pearl are opened
    May we there this friend behold,
Drink with him from living fountains,
    Walk with him the streets of gold.

When life's shattered cords of music
    Shall again be sweetly sung;
Then our hearts with life immortal,
    Shall be young, forever young.

Do you blame me that I loved him?
    If when standing all alone
I cried for bread a careless world
    Pressed to my lips a stone.

Do you blame me that I loved him,
    That my heart beat glad and free,
When he told me in the sweetest tones
    He loved but only me?

Can you blame me that I did not see
    Beneath his burning kiss
The serpent's wiles, nor even hear
    The deadly adder hiss?

Can you blame me that my heart grew cold
    That the tempted, tempter turned;
When he was feted and caressed
    And I was coldly spurned?

Would you blame him, when you draw from me
    Your dainty robes aside,
If he with gilded baits should claim
    Your fairest as his bride?

Would you blame the world if it should press
    On him a civic crown;
And see me struggling in the depth
    Then harshly press me down?

Crime has no sex and yet to-day
    I wear the brand of shame;
Whilst he amid the gay and proud
    Still bears an honored name.

Can you blame me if I've learned to think
    Your hate of vice a sham,
When you so coldly crushed me down
    And then excused the man?

Would you blame me if to-morrow
    The coroner should say,
A wretched girl, outcast, forlorn,
    Has thrown her life away?

Yes, blame me for my downward course,
    But oh! remember well,
Within your homes you press the hand
    That led me down to hell.

I'm glad God's ways are not our ways,
    He does not see as man,
Within His love I know there's room
    For those whom others ban.

I think before His great white throne,
    His throne of spotless light,
That whited sepulchres shall wear
    The hue of endless night.

That I who fell, and he who sinned,
    Shall reap as we have sown;
That each the burden of his loss
    Must bear and bear alone.

No golden weights can turn the scale
    Of justice in His sight;
And what is wrong in woman's life
    In man's cannot be right.

Learning to Read

Very soon the Yankee teachers
    Came down and set up school;
But, oh! how the Rebs did hate it,—
    It was agin' their rule.

Our masters always tried to hide
    Book learning from our eyes;
Knowledge didn't agree with slavery—
    'Twould make us all too wise.

But some of us would try to steal
    A little from the book,
And put the words together,
    And learn by hook or crook.

I remember Uncle Caldwell,
    Who took pot-liquor fat
And greased the pages of his book,
    And hid it in his hat.

And had his master ever seen
    The leaves upon his head,
He'd have thought them greasy papers,
    But nothing to be read.

And there was Mr. Turner's Ben,
    Who heard the children spell,
And picked the words right up by heart,
    And learned to read 'em well.

Well, the Northern folks kept sending
    The Yankee teachers down;
And they stood right up and helped us,
    Though Rebs did sneer and frown.

And, I longed to read my Bible,
    For precious words it said;
But when I begun to learn it,
    Folks just shook their heads,

And said there is no use trying,
    Oh! Chloe, you're too late;
But as I was rising sixty,
    I had no time to wait.

So I got a pair of glasses,
    And straight to work I went,
And never stopped till I could read
    The hymns and Testament.

Then I got a little cabin—
    A place to call my own—
And I felt as independent
    As the queen upon her throne.

EDNA ST. VINCENT MILLAY

She insisted on Vincent, not Edna, and yet, when her first adult poem was published under E. Vincent Millay and a fellow admiring poet assumed the author to be a man, Millay quickly quipped, "I simply will not be 'a brawny male' . . . I cling to my femininity." A prolific lover of women and men, she was happily married for twenty-six years to businessman Eugen Boissevain, a self-identified feminist who gave up his own career to manage the domestic duties so that Millay could spend her time writing. Dramatic, hungry to try everything, she loved the audaciousness of bohemian living in Greenwich Village, but in order to write, she retreated to the isolation of a cabin in a forgotten blueberry field at Steepletop, the farm she and Boissevain cultivated into a home.

In her life, Millay defied definition, shrugging off labels

and expectations so she could live as she saw fit. And yet, ironically, like a firefly in a jar, Millay contained her poetic voice inside the confines of traditional form—mostly the sonnet—while many of her contemporaries were dismantling structure and rhythm and rhyme. But though she toed the line of poetic convention, Millay set about eviscerating strictures of another kind, a liberation she considered far more necessary than the freedom of blank verse. Millay emancipates woman in her poetry. There, woman is free to love whom she loves, free to choose career and artistic expression over love or marriage, free to desire, free to be the one to act on that desire, free to say no to a proposal or good-bye to a lover, free to be powerful and ambitious, free to fail, free to be triumphant—free to be.

And perhaps that is the point of Millay writing in the confines of sonnet form about boundless women. The firefly in a jar commands the singularity of attention more than a field full of them. The jarred firefly, up close, can mesmerize its captor, teach them a new language of light that speaks to the need for freedom for all things, until finally the captor is compelled to let the firefly loose to soar where it will. In life, Edna St. Vincent Millay demanded that freedom, but, more importantly, in her poetry, she hopes we may all find it for ourselves.

The Spring and The Fall

In the spring of the year, in the spring of the year,
I walked the road beside my dear.
The trees were black where the bark was wet.
I see them yet, in the spring of the year.
He broke me a bough of the blossoming peach
That was out of the way and hard to reach.

In the fall of the year, in the fall of the year,
I walked the road beside my dear.
The rooks went up with a raucous trill.
I hear them still, in the fall of the year.
He laughed at all I dared to praise,
And broke my heart, in little ways.

Year be springing or year be falling,

The bark will drip and the birds be calling.

There's much that's fine to see and hear

In the spring of a year, in the fall of a year.

'Tis not love's going hurt my days.

But that it went in little ways.

What Lips My Lips Have Kissed, and Where, and Why

What lips my lips have kissed, and where, and why,
I have forgotten, and what arms have lain
Under my head till morning; but the rain
Is full of ghosts to-night, that tap and sigh
Upon the glass and listen for reply,
And in my heart there stirs a quiet pain
For unremembered lads that not again
Will turn to me at midnight with a cry.
Thus in winter stands the lonely tree,
Nor knows what birds have vanished one by one,
Yet knows its boughs more silent than before:

I cannot say what loves have come and gone,
I only know that summer sang in me
A little while, that in me sings no more.

Thursday

And if I loved you Wednesday,
    Well, what is that to you?
I do not love you Thursday—
    So much is true.

And why you come complaining
    Is more than I can see.
I loved you Wednesday,—yes—but what
    Is that to me?

WILD SWANS

I looked in my heart while the wild swans went over.

And what did I see I had not seen before?

Only a question less or a question more;

Nothing to match the flight of wild birds flying.

Tiresome heart, forever living and dying,

House without air, I leave you and lock your door.

Wild swans, come over the town, come over

The town again, trailing your legs and crying!

I Know I Am but Summer
to Your Heart

I know I am but summer to your heart,
And not the full four seasons of the year;
And you must welcome from another part
Such noble moods as are not mine, my dear.
No gracious weight of golden fruits to sell
Have I, nor any wise and wintry thing;
And I have loved you all too long and well
To carry still the high sweet breast of Spring.
Wherefore I say: O love, as summer goes,
I must be gone, steal forth with silent drums,
That you may hail anew the bird and rose
When I come back to you, as summer comes.
Else will you seek, at some not distant time,
Even your summer in another clime.

I Think I Should Have
Loved You Presently

I think I should have loved you presently,
And given in earnest words I flung in jest;
And lifted honest eyes for you to see,
And caught your hand against my cheek and breast;
And all my pretty follies flung aside
That won you to me, and beneath your gaze,
Naked of reticence and shorn of pride,
Spread like a chart my little wicked ways.
I, that had been to you, had you remained,
But one more waking from a recurrent dream,
Cherish no less the certain stakes I gained,
And walk your memory's halls, austere, supreme,
A ghost in marble of a girl you knew
Who would have loved you in a day or two.

God's World

O world, I cannot hold thee close enough!
  Thy winds, thy wide grey skies!
  Thy mists that roll and rise!
Thy woods, this autumn day, that ache and sag
And all but cry with colour! That gaunt crag
To crush! To lift the lean of that black bluff!
World, World, I cannot get thee close enough!

Long have I known a glory in it all,
  But never knew I this;
  Here such a passion is
As stretcheth me apart. Lord, I do fear
Thou'st made the world too beautiful this year.
My soul is all but out of me, let fall
No burning leaf; prithee, let no bird call.

And You as Well Must Die, Beloved Dust

And you as well must die, beloved dust,
And all your beauty stand you in no stead;
This flawless, vital hand, this perfect head,
This body of flame and steel, before the gust
Of Death, or under his autumnal frost,
Shall be as any leaf, be no less dead
Than the first leaf that fell,—this wonder fled.
Altered, estranged, disintegrated, lost.
Nor shall my love avail you in your hour.
In spite of all my love, you will arise
Upon that day and wander down the air
Obscurely as the unattended flower,
It mattering not how beautiful you were,
Or how beloved above all else that dies.

Elizabeth Barrett Browning

As is often the case with early pioneers taking first steps beyond the accepted norms, Elizabeth Barrett Browning's accomplishments have been overshadowed by the incredible women poets who followed on the path she cut for them. In many ways, Barrett Browning lived a claustrophobic life—trapped, Rapunzel-like, by a controlling father who cherished her as long as she belonged only to him, waylaid by illness, cocooned in her own belief in her "natural ill health," and cut off by apparently extreme social anxiety—she spent much of her time closeted in her room, experiencing little of the world.

And yet, she also benefitted from indulgences and liberties not offered to many women of the time—her wealthy father encouraged her writing and even published her first book of poetry (though he wouldn't allow her name to appear on any of her work until she was thirty-two), her mother read novels with her (fairly shocking for Victorian England), her brother's tutor taught her Latin and Greek and had her read the classics and study philosophy, and her grandmother and uncle left her an inheritance that made her financially secure beyond her father's favor. Her physical limitations (which started early in her teens) also freed her from domestic and social obligations and gave Barrett Browning the time and seclusion to read and write at her leisure.

Influenced at age ten by reading Mary Wollstonecraft's *A Vindication of the Rights of Woman*, and perhaps feeling the boot of patriarchal oppression upon her own neck, Barrett Browning almost immediately began challenging the notions of what a woman poet could and should write about. Ironically, though she's best known for the love sonnets written to Robert Browning, she rejected the idea that a woman should write only about love and religion. Much of her work touches on philosophy and contemporary politics, and even the poems that center on love defy convention. Though steeped in the Victorian morality of her day, Barrett Browning writes of women claiming agency in their lives (most evident in her verse-novel, *Aurora Leigh*), and she exposes the consequences of gender-based double standards. Even her beloved *Sonnets from the Portuguese* flips tradition on its head by having the woman, no longer passive, profess her love to the man.

Given both the obstacles of father and health and the

temptations of an easy, indulgent life, the fact that Elizabeth Barrett Browning wrote at all is impressive. That she wrote of the world and the heart with such affecting power as to amass so many passionate readers and avid critics is astonishing.

How Do I Love Thee?

How do I love thee? Let me count the ways.
I love thee to the depth and breadth and height
My soul can reach, when feeling out of sight
For the ends of Being and ideal Grace.
I love thee to the level of every day's
Most quiet need, by sun and candlelight.
I love thee freely, as men strive for Right;
I love thee purely, as they turn from Praise.
I love with a passion put to use
In my old griefs, and with my childhood's faith.
I love thee with a love I seemed to lose
With my lost saints,—I love thee with the breath,
Smiles, tears, of all my life!—and, if God choose,
I shall but love thee better after death.

LOVE

We cannot live, except thus mutually
We alternate, aware or unaware,
The reflex act of life: and when we bear
Our virtue onward most impulsively,
Most full of invocation, and to be
Most instantly compellant, certes, there
We live most life, whoever breathes most air
And counts his dying years by sun and sea.
But when a soul, by choice and conscience, doth
Throw out her full force on another soul,
The conscience and the concentration both make
mere life, Love. For Life in perfect whole
And aim consummated, is Love in sooth,
As nature's magnet-heat rounds pole with pole.

IF THOU MUST LOVE ME . . .

If thou must love me, let it be for nought
Except for love's sake only. Do not say,
"I love her for her smile—her look—her way
Of speaking gently,—for a trick of thought
That falls in well with mine, and certes brought
A sense of pleasant ease on such a day"—
For these things in themselves, Belovèd, may
Be changed, or change for thee—and love, so wrought,
May be unwrought so. Neither love me for
Thine own dear pity's wiping my cheeks dry:
A creature might forget to weep, who bore
Thy comfort long, and lose thy love thereby!
But love me for love's sake, that evermore
Thou mayst love on, through love's eternity.

DOROTHY PARKER

Dorothy Parker's ashes remained in a filing cabinet in a lawyer's office unclaimed for fifteen years. An odd place to start a biography perhaps, but one she would have likely chosen herself, turning the sad truth into a clever, snarky comment both self-deprecating and highly critical of some other soul, making us all laugh and then letting the bitterness bite us on the way out. It was her modus operandi in life and in her work—charming everyone with her sharp wit, pushing the world away with caustic cynicism, and, in the silent aftermath, making us (and herself) face the truth about loneliness and depression and living in a world that she felt required her to keep her hands balled into fists.

That stance sustained her as she entered the cutthroat and male-dominated world of New York publishing in her early twenties. She skyrocketed to the upper echelons at *Vogue* and *Vanity Fair* and was on the inaugural editorial board of *The New Yorker*. She cofounded the Algonquin Round Table—a weekly gathering of literati that helped to make her quips famous and that she later dissed as irrelevant because none of the truly "great" literary figures, like Hemingway or Faulkner or Fitzgerald, ever paid the group any attention. In addition to pulling strings behind the curtain, Parker published carefully crafted poetry, much of it cloaked in her sardonic voice, and powerful short stories that tend to be more earnest. She once contracted to write a novel and drank a bottle of shoe polish when she missed the deadline.

Dorothy Parker was a woman intentionally untethered from anyone else's expectations but her own, from people, and, sometimes, from her own work. As Lillian Hellman said in Parker's eulogy: "She was part of nobody and nothing except herself; it was this independence of mind and spirit that was her true distinction."

Parties: A Hymn of Hate

I hate Parties;
They bring out the worst in me.

There is the Novelty Affair,
Given by the woman
Who is awfully clever at that sort of thing.
Everybody must come in fancy dress;
They are always eleven Old-Fashioned Girls,
And fourteen Hawaiian gentlemen
Wearing the native costume
Of last season's tennis clothes, with a wreath around
      the neck.

The hostess introduces a series of clean, home games:
Each participant is given a fair chance
To guess the number of seeds in a cucumber,
Or thread a needle against time,

Or see how many names of wild flowers he knows.
Ice cream in trick formations,
And punch like Volstead used to make
Buoy up the players after the mental strain.
You have to tell the hostess that it's a riot,
And she says she'll just die if you don't come to her
      next party—
If only a guarantee went with that!

Then there is the Bridge Festival.
The winner is awarded an arts-and-crafts
      hearth-brush,
And all the rest get garlands of hothouse raspberries.
You cut for partners
And draw the man who wrote the game.
He won't let bygones be bygones;
After each hand
He starts getting personal about your motives in
      leading clubs,
And one word frequently leads to another.

At the next table
You have one of those partners
Who says it is nothing but a game, after all.
He trumps your ace
And tries to laugh it off.
And yet they shoot men like Elwell.

There is the Day in the Country;
It seems more like a week.
All the contestants are wedged into automobiles,
And you are allotted the space between two ladies
Who close in on you.
The party gets a nice early start,
Because everybody wants to make a long day of it—
They get their wish.
Everyone contributes a basket of lunch;
Each person has it all figured out
That no one else will think of bringing hard-boiled eggs.

There is intensive picking of dogwood,
And no one is quite sure what poison ivy is like;
They find out the next day.
Things start off with a rush.
Everybody joins in the old songs,
And points out cloud effects,
And puts in a good word for the colour of the grass.

But after the first fifty miles,
Nature doesn't go over so big,
And singing belongs to the lost arts.
There is a slight spurt on the homestretch,
And everyone exclaims over how beautiful the lights of
        the city look—
I'll say they do.

And there is the informal little Dinner Party;
The lowest form of taking nourishment.
The man on your left draws diagrams with a fork,
Illustrating the way he is going to have a new sun-
      parlour built on;
And the one on your right
Explains how soon business conditions will better,
      and why.

When the more material part of the evening is over,
You have your choice of listening to the Harry Lauder
      records,
Or having the hostess hem you in
And show you the snapshots of the baby they took last
      summer.

Just before you break away,
You mutter something to the host and hostess
About sometime soon you must have them over—
Over your dead body.

I hate Parties;
They bring out the worst in me.

BALLADE AT THIRTY-FIVE

This, no song of an ingénue,
This, no ballad of innocence;
This, the rhyme of a lady who
Followed ever her natural bents.
This, a solo of sapience,
This, a chantey of sophistry,
This, the sum of experiments,—
I loved them until they loved me.

Decked in garments of sable hue,
Daubed with ashes of myriad Lents,
Wearing shower bouquets of rue,
Walk I ever in penitence.
Oft I roam, as my heart repents,

Through God's acre of memory,
Marking stones, in my reverence,
"I loved them until they loved me."

Pictures pass me in long review,—
Marching columns of dead events.
I was tender, and, often, true;
Ever a prey to coincidence.
Always knew I the consequence;
Always saw what the end would be.
We're as Nature has made us—hence
I loved them until they loved me.

PHILLIS WHEATLEY

*P*hillis Wheatley was a woman with the world on her
shoulders.

Kidnapped from her home in Africa as a young girl, shoved
into a ship and forced to survive the horrors of the Middle
Passage, sold into slavery in Boston in 1761, she was bought by
John Wheatley for his wife, Susanna—by all accounts benevo-
lent masters but masters all the same. Phillis Wheatley's quick
mind and eagerness to learn soon caught the attention of her
mistress. Susanna Wheatley and her daughter, Mary, undertook
Wheatley's education in reading, writing, religious instruc-
tion, and eventually Latin and the classics. Her first poem was
published to acclaim on both continents just seven years later—
which is when the hopes of all enslaved peoples fell on her back.

In efforts to procure the funds to publish a book of poetry, they had to prove that Phillis Wheatley had indeed written the verses, and so a committee of eighteen white men, mostly Harvard graduates and slave owners, questioned the teenager. As Henry Louis Gates Jr. argues in *The Trials of Phillis Wheatley,* "Essentially, she was auditioning for the humanity of the entire African people." She won.

Poems on Various Subjects, Religious and Moral (1773) was the first book ever published by an African American woman, and Wheatley obtained her freedom from John and Susanna shortly thereafter. A sad testament to the evils of oppression, the woman who laid the cornerstone for African American literature died alone in a boardinghouse where she scrubbed floors, abandoned by her husband, a dead infant by her side, and was buried in an unmarked grave.

On Imagination

Thy various works, imperial queen, we see,
    How bright their forms! how deck'd with pomp
      by thee!
Thy wond'rous acts in beauteous order stand,
And all attest how potent is thine hand.

    From Helicon's refulgent heights attend,
Ye sacred choir, and my attempts befriend:
To tell her glories with a faithful tongue,
Ye blooming graces, triumph in my song.

    Now here, now there, the roving Fancy flies,
Till some lov'd object strikes her wand'ring eyes,
Whose silken fetters all the senses bind,
And soft captivity involves the mind.

Imagination! who can sing thy force?
Or who describe the swiftness of thy course?
Soaring through air to find the bright abode,
Th' empyreal palace of the thund'ring God,
We on thy pinions can surpass the wind,
And leave the rolling universe behind:
From star to star the mental optics rove,
Measure the skies, and range the realms above.
There in one view we grasp the mighty whole,
Or with new worlds amaze th' unbounded soul.

Though Winter frowns to Fancy's raptur'd eyes
The fields may flourish, and gay scenes arise;
The frozen deeps may break their iron bands,
And bid their waters murmur o'er the sands.
Fair Flora may resume her fragrant reign,
And with her flow'ry riches deck the plain;
Sylvanus may diffuse his honours round,
And all the forest may with leaves be crown'd:
Show'rs may descend, and dews their gems disclose,
And nectar sparkle on the blooming rose.

Such is thy pow'r, nor are thine orders vain,
O thou the leader of the mental train:
In full perfection all thy works are wrought,
And thine the sceptre o'er the realms of thought.

Before thy throne the subject-passions bow,

Of subject-passions sov'reign ruler thou;

At thy command joy rushes on the heart,

And through the glowing veins the spirits dart.

Fancy might now her silken pinions try

To rise from earth, and sweep th' expanse on high:

From Tithon's bed now might Aurora rise,

Her cheeks all glowing with celestial dies,

While a pure stream of light o'erflows the skies.

The monarch of the day I might behold,

And all the mountains tipt with radiant gold,

But I reluctant leave the pleasing views,

Which Fancy dresses to delight the Muse;

Winter austere forbids me to aspire,

And northern tempests damp the rising fire;

They chill the tides of Fancy's flowing sea,

Cease then, my song, cease the unequal lay.

An Hymn to the Morning

Attend my lays, ye ever honour'd nine,
Assist my labours, and my strains refine;
In smoothest numbers pour the notes along,
For bright Aurora now demands my song.

Aurora hail, and all the thousand dies,
Which deck thy progress through the vaulted skies:
The morn awakes, and wide extends her rays,
On ev'ry leaf the gentle zephyr plays;
Harmonious lays the feather'd race resume,
Dart the bright eye, and shake the painted plume.

Ye shady groves, your verdant gloom display
To shield your poet from the burning day:
Calliope awake the sacred lyre,

While thy fair sisters fan the pleasing fire:
The bow'rs, the gales, the variegated skies
In all their pleasures in my bosom rise.

See in the east th' illustrious king of day!
His rising radiance drives the shades away—
But Oh! I feel his fervid beams too strong,
And scarce begun, concludes th' abortive song.

A Farewel to America.

To Mrs. S. W.

I.

Adieu, New-England's smiling meads,

　　Adieu, the flow'ry plain:

I leave thine op'ning charms, O spring,

　　And tempt the roaring main.

II.

In vain for me the flow'rets rise,

　　And boast their gaudy pride,

While here beneath the northern skies

　　I mourn for health deny'd.

III.

Celestial maid of rosy hue,

　　O let me feel thy reign!

I languish till thy face I view,

　　Thy vanish'd joys regain.

IV.

Susanna mourns, nor can I bear

    To see the crystal show'r,

Or mark the tender falling tear

    At sad departure's hour;

V.

Not unregarding can I see

    Her soul with grief opprest:

But let no sighs, no groans for me,

    Steal from her pensive breast.

VI.

In vain the feather'd warblers sing,

    In vain the garden blooms,

And on the bosom of the spring

    Breathes out her sweet perfumes.

VII.

While for Britannia's distant shore

    We sweep the liquid plain,

And with astonish'd eyes explore

    The wide-extended main.

VIII.

Lo! Health appears! celestial dame!

    Complacent and serene,

With Hebe's mantle o'er her Frame,

    With soul-delighting mein.

IX.

To mark the vale where London lies
      With misty vapours crown'd,
Which cloud Aurora's thousand dyes,
      And veil her charms around.

X.

Why, Phoebus, moves thy car so slow?
      So slow thy rising ray?
Give us the famous town to view,
      Thou glorious king of day!

XI.

For thee, Britannia, I resign
      New-England's smiling fields;
To view again her charms divine,
      What joy the prospect yields!

XII.

But thou! Temptation hence away,
      With all thy fatal train,
Nor once seduce my soul away,
      By thine enchanting strain.

XIII.

Thrice happy they, whose heav'nly shield
      Secures their souls from harms,
And fell Temptation on the field
      Of all its pow'r disarms!

BIBLIOGRAPHY

Alcott, Louisa May. *Her Life, Letters, and Journals.* Edited by Ednah D. Cheney. Boston: Little, Brown, 1898.

Brontë, Charlotte. *Jane Eyre.* 4th ed. New York: Norton Critical Edition, 2016.

Campbell, Donna. "An Edith Wharton Chronology." *The Edith Wharton Society.* https://public.wsu.edu/~campbelld/wharton/wchron.htm.

Gates, Henry Louis, Jr. *The Trials of Phillis Wheatley.* New York: Civitas Books, 2003.

Harper, Frances Ellen Watkins. "Address to Eleventh National Women's Rights Convention in New York, 1866." Iowa State University Archives of Women's Political Communication. https://awpc.cattcenter.iastate.edu/2017/03/21/we-are-all-bound-up-together-may-1866/.

Heger, Constantin. Quoted in Elizabeth Gaskell. *The Life of Charlotte Brontë.* Harmondsworth, England: Penguin, 1975.

Hellman, Lillian. Eulogy for Dorothy Parker. Quoted in Richard Moody. *Lillian Hellman Playwright.* New York: Bobbs-Merrill, 1972.

Millay, Edna St. Vincent. Letter to Witter Bynner and Arthur
    Davison Ficke. Quoted in Daniel Mark Epstein. *What Lips My
    Lips Have Kissed: The Loves and Love Poems of Edna St. Vincent
    Millay.* New York: Henry Holt, 2001.

Stein, Gertrude. *Everybody's Autobiography.* New York: Vintage
    Books, 1973.

Wheelwright, Laetitia. Letter as quoted in "Emily in Brussels." *The
    Brussels Brontë Group.* www.thebrusselsbrontegroup.org/emily
    -bronte-in-brussels/emily-in-brussels-2/.

DANA CHAMBLEE CARPENTER

*D*ana Chamblee Carpenter is both a writer and an academic. She is the author of the award-winning historical fantasy series: The Bohemian Trilogy. The first book in the series, *Bohemian Gospel*, introduces Mouse, a young woman searching for her purpose in the world. *Publishers Weekly* said: "Mouse is both strong and vulnerable, constantly struggling with the dark legacy of her father, her own powers, and her efforts to be a good person." Books two and three, *The Devil's Bible* and *Book of the Just*, continue Mouse's struggle to come to terms with her past and to accept who she is. Dr. Chamblee Carpenter also teaches creative writing and American literature at Lipscomb University in Nashville, Tennessee, where she lives with her husband and two children.